IS THERE A REAL CURSE ON STATS'S FAVORITE TEAM?

Billee lowered his voice. "I fear there may very well be a new Red Sox curse afoot."

"Oh, you don't really mean that, do you?" Stats could feel his heart plump up and flutter out a double beat.

The pitcher narrowed his eyes. "As far as I'm concerned, we'll find out tonight. This game will be the real test. If the momentum shifts, if things start to turn around and go my way, then I'll say, okay, maybe it will start to all even out. No harm, no foul balls. But if not, then—"

He took another bite, looking high over Stats's lucky 2007 Red Sox cap, far into the clouds.

Stats turned around and looked up, too, but didn't see much. "Then what?" he asked.

Billee chewed slowly, pondering.

"Then it'll be up to guys like you and me to stop this new curse."

OTHER BOOKS YOU MAY ENJOY

FENWAY FEVER

JOHN H. RITTER

PUFFIN BOOKS
An Imprint of Penguin Group (USA) Inc.

PUFFIN BOOKS
Published by the Penguin Group
Penguin Young Readers Group, 345 Hudson Street, New York, New York 10014, U.S.A.
Penguin Group (Canada), 90 Eglinton Avenue East, Suite 700, Toronto, Ontario M4P 2Y3, Canada
(a division of Pearson Penguin Canada Inc.)
Penguin Books Ltd, 80 Strand, London WC2R 0RL, England
Penguin Ireland, 25 St Stephen's Green, Dublin 2, Ireland (a division of Penguin Books Ltd)
Penguin Group (Australia), 707 Collins Street, Melbourne, Victoria 3008, Australia
(a division of Pearson Australia Group Pty Ltd)
Penguin Books India Pvt Ltd, 11 Community Centre, Panchsheel Park, New Delhi–110 017, India
Penguin Group (NZ), 67 Apollo Drive, Rosedale, Auckland 0632, New Zealand
(a division of Pearson New Zealand Ltd)
Penguin Books, Rosebank Office Park, 181 Jan Smuts Avenue,
Parktown North 2193, South Africa
Penguin China, B7 Jiaming Center, 27 East Third Ring Road North,
Chaoyang District, Beijing 100020, China

Penguin Books Ltd, Registered Offices: 80 Strand, London WC2R 0RL, England

First published in the United States of America by Philomel Books,
a division of Penguin Young Readers Group, 2012
Published by Puffin Books, a member of Penguin Young Readers Group, 2013

3 5 7 9 10 8 6 4 2

THE LIBRARY OF CONGRESS HAS CATALOGED THE PHILOMEL BOOKS EDITION AS FOLLOWS:
Ritter, John H., date.
Fenway fever / John H. Ritter. p. cm.
Summary: Twelve-year-old Alfredo "Stats" Pagano and Boston Red Sox pitcher Billee Orbitt
work together to break a potential curse at Fenway Park.
ISBN 978-0-399-24665-4(hc)
1. Boston Red Sox (Baseball team)—Juvenile fiction.
2. Fenway Park (Boston, Mass.)—Juvenile fiction.
[1. Boston Red Sox (Baseball team)—Fiction. 2. Fenway Park (Boston, Mass.)—Fiction.
3. Baseball—Fiction. 4. Blessing and cursing—Fiction. 5. Boston (Mass.)—Fiction.]
I. Title. PZ7.R5148Fe 2012 [Fic]—dc23 2011037113

Puffin Books ISBN 978-0-14-242491-9

Printed in the United States of America

Edited by Michael Green.
Design by Amy Wu. Text set in Life LT Std.

FENWAY FEVER

This one's for my big sis,
Dr. Carol Pierce,
who altered her life to watch over, guide, and sacrifice
for her three young brothers when our mother died.
And she watches over still . . .
with love, John

And for Michael Green,
longtime true believer
my editor, anchor, brother, friend,
and pilot once again
without whom there would be no sky
con gratitud infinita, juan

ACKNOWLEDGMENTS

I particularly wish to thank: Dr. Janis Flint-Ferguson of Gordon College and her husband, Rex, for my baptism long ago upon the oakwood seats of Fenway and for hosting many happy returns; Vanessa Crooks, for her expert assistance over the years in organizing my forays in and about New England; Tamra Tuller, a wise and vibrant editor with high patience and a keen eye; Anthony Wing for his thoughtful insights on an early draft; Marlie Allen for homemade ice cream and emotional support; Kannon Allen for his creative sparks and contagious can-do spirit; and most of all, I want to thank Cheryl, my bride of now forty years, who interprets the world for me in both concrete and angelic ways, as befits a teacher of both English and Yoga, beyond a doubt the Pegasus of my life.

with love, John H. Ritter
Spring of 2012

"ONCE YOU HAVE TASTED FLIGHT,
YOU WILL FOREVER WALK
THE EARTH WITH YOUR EYES TURNED SKYWARD,
FOR THERE YOU HAVE BEEN,
AND THERE YOU WILL ALWAYS LONG TO RETURN."
—Leonardo da Vinci

"THE GOAL OF LIFE IS TO MAKE YOUR HEARTBEAT
MATCH THE BEAT OF THE UNIVERSE,
TO MATCH YOUR NATURE WITH NATURE."
—Joseph Campbell

"O! FOR A HORSE WITH WINGS!"
—William Shakespeare, *Cymbeline*

CHAPTER 0

*It was the last of times, it was
the first of times.*

*It was the old ending. It was
the new big inning.*

*It was the magical year of
2012.*

*And among the fens and bogs
of Boston town, something was
amiss . . .*

Let's face it, baseball fans, no ballpark on earth holds as much legendary drama, karma, curses, heartbreak, and hope as Fenway Park at Number 4 Yawkey Way in Boston. Sure, you got your Wrigley Field in Chicago town with its ivy-covered walls or the old coliseum out Oakland way or the big blue sea of seats at Dodger Stadium in L.A. A lot of greats have passed through their gates, no doubt, but when it comes to legends, no ballyard anywhere holds a candlestick to the ol' Fen.

And no one knows that better than Alfredo Carl "Stats" Pagano, who's spent half his life (that's six out of twelve years or, more precisely, 73.5 out of 147 months or, expressed as a batting average, an even .500 of this baseball lover's lifetime) gathering stats and data on the Boston Red Sox and their quirky hundred-year-old ballfield.

And during Fenway Park's hundredth anniversary, in that legendary year of 2012, the place went bonkers. Banners flapped from bridges. Billboards told the tale.

100 YEARS OF CHEERS AND TEARS! they read. CATCH FENWAY FEVER! others proclaimed. IT'S A FAN-DEMIC!

Old pros and Hollywood celebs alike recorded JumboTron testimonials recalling what the ballpark had meant to them. Centennial posters hung in bookstore windows, while "First Fen-tury" flags adorned the walls of sports bars everywhere.

Ah, but deep beneath all the festivity and hooplicity, there crept the foreshadows of a calamity that no one in town, from the sea captains of Gloucester to the philosophers of Harvard University, seemed to notice.

Luckily, one small and brilliant boy and one rather strange Red Sox pitcher saw the signs and decided to step up to the plate and swing away.

What happened next was out of this world.

1

The pre-game street scene rivering past Papa Pagano's Red Sox Red Hots hot dog stand, just outside the gates of Fenway Park, had grown loud and tense.

A certain fear hung in the air.

"No, no, I'm telling you," one Red Sox fan bellowed at his buddy. "Orbitt should not be pitching. After four straight fiascos, why is he starting? He should be in the bull pen. And I mean the one down in Pawtucket."

"Like I said before, Mr. Beer-for-Brains, he's had some weird luck, is all. The Spacebird is still the man. You'll see."

"Weird is right. I got twenty bucks that says Billee Orbitt, the space *cadet*, won't get out of the first inning."

"You're on!"

All afternoon, from his station at the back of the hand-crafted wrought-iron hot dog stand on Yawkey Way, statistical whiz kid Alfredo "Stats" Pagano had taken these friendly quarrels in stride.

Tonight's match, the third of a four-game series pitting the Boston Red Sox against their archrivals, the New York Yankees, had the streets and bars around Fenway Park packed and punchy, even three hours before game time.

"Hey, was that guy right?" asked Pops Pagano, a burly man with a husky voice. He plopped a fresh-grilled Smokey Joe wood-fired dog onto a toasted bun. "Billee's on the hill tonight?"

"Last I heard," said Stats, who tended two steamy kettles next to Pops's grill. "Unless they make another last-minute change."

And even though the Red Sox had dropped the first two games to the so-called Evil Empire from New York—or maybe because of it—Stats could hardly wait to head inside and catch the action.

He took a second Smokey Joe from Pops and began to wrap them both. "They skipped over Billee last time around. So he should be up."

His older brother, Mark, who at fifteen towered head and elbows over Stats, called from the cash register up front, "Skipped over him? They *sank* him just because of a little bad luck."

"Ahh," Pops growled as he slapped a half dozen more hot dogs onto the grill. "He's a tough kid. He'll bounce back."

Stats boxed the Smokey Joes and slid them forward.

Mark caught the box and passed it to a shirtless fanatic everyone called Announcer Bouncer—a guy with a voice so loud you could hear it from home plate to the Green Monster seats high above left field. Rainbowing across his bouncing belly, he'd painted BILLEEZ BOYZ! in white, blue, and red.

"Here you go, Bounce," said Mark. "See you inside."

"I'll put it on my calendar," he barked.

Mark shook his head, laughing. "Get outta here. Next!"

Up stepped a white-haired man in a rumpled dark business suit, sans tie. "I'll have two Teddy Ballgamers, kraut, no mustard, two Smokey Joes, mustard, no ketchup, three Chili Billees, and one foot-long Hit Dog with everything."

Pops, in his high-top chef's hat, looked up from his grill. "Got it, buddy! Hey, is that for here or to go?"

The man arched his eyebrows. "What?"

Pops was always using that line on new customers, just to bust their chops. *Here or to go?* What could the guy say?

Mark waved his hand. "I'll take that as a 'to go.'"

Stats had already grabbed two Smokeys and set them aside, then he fished two regular dogs and a footer from his saltwater kettle. He put the regulars inside fresh Boston rolls atop blue paper sheets stamped "Teddy Ballgamer" and dropped the footer onto a soft steamed bun.

Next, Stats sprinkled onions and diced tomatoes on the foot-long Hit Dog, which actually measured 12.5 inches, because, as the sign for this one promised, YOU GET *MO* FOR YOUR MONEY.

He slid all five down the side counter to Mark, who dumped a ladle of sauerkraut on the Ballgamers, finished wrapping them, and started a box.

"Waiting on the Billees," called Stats.

"Can't rush magic," said Pops.

Stats knew that, as did all loyal Red Sox fans. Magic can take a long time.

It had taken until 2004, in fact, for the Sox to win their first Major League World Series in eighty-six years. And they did so in magical Red Sox fashion, mounting a surge from three games down in the League Championship Series to stop the New York Yankees in seven (becoming the first team to ever do such a thing), then swept the St. Louis Cardinals in four to win the World Series and break baseball's longest-running bad-luck streak, the legendary *Curse of the Bambino*.

Sparked by the sale of Red Sox ace pitcher and long-ball hitter Babe Ruth, the Great Bambino, to the Yankees (of all teams!) way back in 1919, this phenomenal curse had spanned several generations, breaking millions of hearts along the way.

But those days were long gone now, Stats felt sure.

Seeing Mark take the customer's money, Stats started his mental stopwatch—a game he often played while waiting on Pops. Mark punched the register, scratched out the change from his coin bins, added a few bills, and handed it all over. Then, using his hip, he clanged the cash drawer shut and pulled the food box close, shot a thick river of mustard on both Smokeys, spooned a scoop of relish on the footer, added ketchup and mustard, and folded each into their wrappers.

All in nine seconds! Not a record, thought Stats, but still remarkable by any measure.

Being younger, and a bit less coordinated in the hand-and-eye department, Stats never begrudged Mark his dexterity and athleticism. Having been born with a damaged heart, Stats had long ago resigned himself to the world of mental gymnastics. The only thing that really irked him was when people would note that he was "rather small" for a boy his age.

Well, maybe he was, which any boy born with a balky heart might be. Still, he regarded such comments as "rather rude" and had learned to respond politely, but firmly.

"Actually, I'm not small for my age," he would say. "The truth is, I'm rather old for my height."

This, he found, usually shut the errant observers rather up.

He gave each of his kettles a stir. In one, he boiled several kinds of hot dogs in saltwater brine. In the other, he stewed fresh organic chili, which he ladled onto the all-veggie Chili Billee dogs, filling them FULL OF BEANS, as promised, JUST LIKE THEIR NAMESAKE.

Resting his stainless steel ladle against the black kettle rim, Stats slipped his hand into his front pocket and anxiously fingered his two game day tickets. Still there. His heart boomed.

These, you see, were not your ordinary everyday baseball passes. These were family heirloom tickets—*season tickets*— seats his grandfather, Papa Pagano, founder of the Red Sox Red Hots stand, first purchased for himself and his new American bride seventy-two years ago. Front-row, field-level seats, just past third base on the edge of the outfield grass.

"Heaven on earth," Stats liked to call them.

Some days, Pops might pass the tickets along to various

associates of the family hot dog stand, and sometimes they might end up in the offering plate at St. Francis of Assisi's or dropped through the mail slot of a homeless shelter in Southie. But today, the seats belonged to him and Mark.

And on such days, as soon as they heard "The Star-Spangled Banner" from their stations at the sidewalk stand in the shadow of the ruddy brick walls of Fenway, they'd slip off their long white aprons, wipe the mustard from their hands, sing out, "See ya, Pops," and dash inside.

Needless to say, Stats and Mark Pagano were, by all decent and acceptable standards, the luckiest boys on planet earth.

This, however, was about to change.

CHAPTER 2

As the afternoon wore on, Stats tended his kettles while Pops did his best to hustle up customers from the throng moving down the street.

"Get-cha Red Sox Red Hots right hee-ya!"

Pops Pagano sang his Bostonian-laden incantation loud and strong, as if he were a priest calling to his flock.

"Hey, getcha Red Hots, now."

In fact, Stats often thought that if Father McNamara would hire Pops on Sundays to stand in the St. Francis bell tower calling the parishioners to Holy Communion, the church would be packed at every service. Although, knowing Pops, the call would be more like, "Getcha red wine hee-ya! Hey, now, fresh white wayfahs hee-ya!"

That approach would, most likely, garner a few complaints at St. Francis, but it was perfect for Papa Pagano's.

And business at the sidewalk stand was booming.

"Here's four more," said Pops, depositing four Chili Billees on toasted buns onto the workspace in front of Stats, who, in turn, smothered them in chili, wrapped them into their green paper sheets, and sent them sliding toward the front.

Mark stuffed the order into a box. "Put a jalapeño in it?" he asked.

"Go ahead," said the man, who stuck a five-dollar tip into an old pickle jar, which was guarded by a stubble-bearded Kevin Youkilis bobble-head doll.

"Thanks!" called Mark. "Next!"

"Hit me with your best shot, Stat Man."

That order did not come from the front of the line, but from a curly-headed young man standing just outside the booth next to Stats. He was wearing aviator sunglasses, a white cowboy hat with a Red Sox logo, a blue Red Sox hoodie with the hood up, purplish tie-dyed drawstring pants, and white moccasins. To Stats, the guy appeared to be a cross between a '78 "Buffalo Head" and an '04 curse-breaking "Idiot"—two of the more colorful eras of Red Sox players.

However, beneath this way-out attire stood Boston's number three starting pitcher and their number one star attraction. Although, as far as Stats was concerned, this goofball lefty's biggest claim to fame was that he, Billee Orbitt, was the only active Red Sox player to have a Papa Pagano's hot dog named in his honor.

"My best shot," said Stats, "has your name written all over it." He snagged two red-hot freshly charred veggie dogs off of Pops's grill.

"What the heck are you doing out here on a game day, Billee? Aren't you starting?"

Mark and Pops kept working, as they usually did at these moments, to let the two "kids" talk. Billee Orbitt frequently visited Papa Pagano's on his off days to grab a few dogs, a good-luck ritual he had begun last year—which he claimed "worked like a snake charm"—but Stats could not ever recall him stopping by on a day he was scheduled to pitch.

He pointed at the pitcher's weird clothes. "You got your uniform on under that?"

"Half of it." Billee grinned, looking himself over. "Just trying to shake things up a bit and break my routine. Besides, I'm starving. Red Sox have no food left in there."

"Shake what things up?"

"You kidding? Look, I've lost four in a row, and my ERA's still around 3.20. What does that tell you?"

Stats thought a moment. "It's 3.13, actually, but what's wrong with that? Allowing three runs per game is not a bad average at all."

"I agree, which proves I'm throwing about as good as I ever have, with nothing but a lousy one-and-four record to show for it. Last game, for example, I was zoned, baby. Zoom, ziggy, zoom." He wing-waddled his hand through the air. "But it wasn't enough. And not only that, we have gone from four games in front of the Yankees to one game behind in, what, ten days? We're not that bad of a team, Stat Man. Something else is going on."

"Like what?"

"I have to believe there are some outside forces at work here. After all, it's *2012*."

Stats had heard that talk before. Actually, a lot of people believed this year, 2012, was supposed to be earth-changing— maybe even the end of the world as we knew it.

"Hasn't been all that bad," offered Stats, who put very little stock in the whole 2012 doom-and-gloom scenario.

To be honest, Stats, as well as zillions of devoted members of Red Sox Nation, preferred to see it this way: If the holy game of baseball was coming to an end during the year of the Fenway Park Centennial, then they figured it would be only fitting that their Sox should win not just the 2012 American League pennant, but the world's last World Series to boot.

"Hey, you win tonight," Stats continued, "and we stop the slide. We're back even with the Yanks, with a chance to split the series tomorrow and regain first place. Besides, the last time you pitched, what was it? You left in the fifth, game tied four– four, right? Then a seeing-eye single and a pop flare scores two? Not your fault we lost. In baseball that stuff happens. But it always evens out over time. And I got the stats to prove it."

He grinned widely.

Billee shook his head. "Wish that were true, Stat Man. But this year's different. It's not just a bad bounce here, bloop hit there. A boot, a bobble. Most of the time, that stuff does even out. But this is pure bad luck. And it's all one-sided. Plus, it's only getting worse. One thing goes wrong, then two, then three.

Before you know it, I get hung with an 'L,' the team goes down-hill, and, buddy"—he waggled his cowboy hat—"it's driving me ba-zerko."

Ah, thought Stats, so that's what does it. But he decided not to say anything. He did have to admit, though, Billee had a point.

Last year, during his rookie season, Billee was baseball's star attraction, a twenty-one-year-old phenom. People packed the parks in every city he pitched just to watch his ninety-three-mph "buckler ball" buckle a batter's knees, his "dipster ball" dip and dash, and his world-famous slo-mo "leaflutz" pitch flutter like a falling leaf, while hitters flailed away, smacking nothing but air.

The fans also loved to see Billee's herky-jerky merry-go-round windup, known as the "Lefty Looey," since it reminded the Boston faithful of a left-handed version of former Sox pitching great Luis Tiant.

Of course, it also helped that Billee was a local boy, born in Worcester, Mass., and raised in Northborough. In his year at triple-A Pawtucket, he was tagged the "Worcester Rooster," as much for his habit of scratching up the mound between innings as the fact that around here, regardless of spelling, those two words actually rhyme. Later on, fans dubbed him the Space-bird, partly because of the rooster tag and partly because of his often-stated dream to one day fly through space and visit his ancestors.

Needless to say, the loony (as in *lunar*) left-hander became an overnight fan favorite. But as most folks would agree, last year ended on a sour note, and Billee's star was beginning to fade.

He grabbed the first chili dog Stats set on the counter, then walked over to pitch a wadded-up twenty into the tip jar. Billee never had to pay for his food—one of Pops's rules—but he always left a generous tip.

"Hey, Pops!" called Billee, holding his chili dog high. "Have I ever told you this? Your hot dogs are a legend in their own brine."

Pops threw his head back and roared. "About a thousand times, you Wiener schnitzel. Now, move along." He pointed in Mark's direction with his silver tongs. "Look how slow the line's going with you standing around."

Despite being incognito, the gangly, animated pitcher had been quickly identified by several fans, who started bunching up at the counter to gawk. The purple pants may have been a giveaway, if not the deerskin pouch full of herbs (mixed with Fenway Park grass trimmings) dangling from his neck.

Billee, however, simply scooped up the next chili dog and sent a wave to everyone as they, in turn, wished him luck. Then he began his customary stroll toward a small nook in the brick wall behind the sidewalk stand, where he and Stats often conferred. Stats slipped under the countertop to follow.

"All right, Stat Man," said Billee. "Status report. What've you uncovered so far?"

As he straightened up, Stats felt his heart flutter. Closing his fist, he tapped his chest, then coughed. It was one of the strategies he had discovered to overcome the swelling surge of palpitations he sometimes felt. The feeling left.

"Thought you'd never ask, Billee. I've had the whole Stat Pack helping me all week, and there's one thing we came up with that you might be very interested in."

Billee's upside-down traffic cone of a goatee sprouted a full toothy grin from somewhere inside. "That's why I hired you, kid."

"Hired" was stretching it. But last week Billee had asked Stats to research a few things, and, as usual, Stats was happy to help.

His task was to scour the scorebooks and compile data on such things as uncompleted double plays that led to a run being scored; bad hop, "seeing-eye," or fluke hits that scored key runs; and passed balls or wild pitches that advanced runners who later scored. Billee labeled these "bad-luck runs." He wanted to know if, as he suspected, the Sox had lost more close games because of bad-luck runs (BLRs) than other teams up to this point—the first six weeks of the season.

"Okay, so, I sorted through all the data on all of the teams, and the Red Sox have already had six BLR losses this year. Which is more than any other team we know of."

Stats paused while Billee chomped down into his chili dog and leaned against the ancient wall covered with posters shouting FENWAY FEVER! 100° AND RISING! He nodded.

Stats went on. "The interesting thing is, four of those losses happened when you pitched."

"Well," said Billee. "Maybe I'm not so crazy after all."

Again, Stats thought it best not to comment. But he did feel compelled to inject an element of logic.

"Billee, I know what you're thinking. You gotta remember what I said, though. In the long run, statistically speaking, there really is no such thing as good luck or bad. It pretty much evens out over time."

Billee lowered an eyebrow and cocked his head. "And like I say, this is different. Trust me, Stat Man. I'm *tuned in* to stuff like this. They don't call me Spacebird for nothing." He set his fists against his temples, then extended both pointing fingers and wiggled them. "Voom, zoom."

He winked, then grew serious. "Okay, bud, here's what I'd like you to do next. Start tuning in to the vibe around here. Find out all you can about anything around this ballpark that could've knocked things out of whack."

"Out of whack?" said Stats. "Like what?"

"Like anything. With all the recent renovations, who knows? Renaming the .406 Club could've done it, replacing all the solid oak seats with plastic might've done it, or even installing those three new HD video boards. And it might not be just one thing. They all add up, you know."

"Add up to what?"

"To a new balance. Which means the old balance we had back in '04 and '07 may be long gone. And if that's the case . . ." Billee lowered his voice. "I fear there may very well be a new Red Sox curse afoot."

"Oh, you don't really mean that, do you?" Stats could feel his heart plump up and flutter out a double beat.

The pitcher narrowed his eyes. "As far as I'm concerned, we'll find out tonight. This game will be the real test. If the momentum shifts, if things start to turn around and go my way, then I'll say, okay, maybe it will start to all even out. No harm, no foul balls. But if not, then—"

He took another bite, looking high over Stats's lucky 2007 Red Sox cap, far into the clouds.

Stats turned around and looked up, too, but didn't see much. "Then what?" he asked.

Billee chewed slowly, pondering.

"Then it'll be up to guys like you and me to stop this new curse."

CHAPTER 3

After an exhausting three hours, the action at Papa Pagano's had finally slowed to a "one-man stand," as Pops called it. Stats held wet towels in each hand like mitts, mopping up the countertops and storage bins, while Mark worked a wire brush over the still-smoldering grill.

As if on cue, Stats could hear the legendary Celtic rock band Dropkick Murphys begin singing the national anthem inside the ballpark, and Pops waved his hand.

"Get outta here," he commanded.

The boys tossed their towels into the linen box behind the counter, then pulled off their aprons and slung them in, too. Mark lifted the escape hatch, snatching his ballpark glove off its hook. Stats grabbed his scorebook. And they both hustled away.

Now, Pops was a great Red Sox fan, too, don't let anyone tell you different. Long before Stats was even born, Pops had attended games religiously, all the way through the 2007 World Series. Along with Mama Pagano.

When she got sick, however, everything normal came to a halt. When she died, everything changed.

These days, Pops was happy just to root from the outside, watch his tiny TV, listen for the roars, and know that he did not have to walk down that long aisle of narrow steps that leads to the front row of section 71. Nor did he have to pause at the foot of the aisleway, to see one seat waiting for him and the other one empty.

In the top of the first, Billee started his routine, which would tend to get replayed on the scoreboard and for the fans at home from time to time. First he tramped around the mound, scratching and smoothing the dirt. Then he turned his back to the catcher and held the ball to his face, saying something encouraging to it. Finally, he began warming up.

As was his custom, with each pitch Billee spun fully around, nodding at the infielders, before he uncoiled like a striking snake to deliver the ball to the plate. The fans loved it and responded with hoots and whistles after each toss.

When catcher Burlin Fiske received the final warm-up pitch, he rifled the ball to second, where it was zipped around the horn, only to be flipped ten feet high by Wadell Fens, at third, so Billee could snatch the "falling star" bare-handed. Tucking his glove under his arm, he then stalked around the mound, slapping and rubbing the ball with his left palm. Satisfied finally with the "feel" of the situation, Billee stepped to the rubber and looked in for a sign.

For the first hour, this highly hyped game between the top

two AL East Division teams became a pitchers' duel, with no score through four.

Billee had to be happy. He looked unhittable. Stats could feel his heart calm and his breathing grow strong.

When Flasher Gordon, the Yankees' leadoff man in the top of the fifth, went down on strikes, everyone rose. What a relief, thought Stats, to see the fans supporting Billee Orbitt once again. Lately the snarls and sneers had grown proportionate to the Red Sox's slide out of first place. Last night, when things got rough for young True Denton on the mound, Stats had witnessed several in the crowd become a strange gang of hostiles, their faces rife with anger.

"Our team is our team," Pops had always said. "Win or lose, they come to play and play their best. So why turn on them?"

Mark could, of course, offer a few reasons why, but Stats would always counter and help Pops hold his ground.

The next batter chopped one to the second sacker, Dusty Doretta, who promptly swept it up and fired to Sandiego Gunsalvo at first for out number two.

After Billee got ahead on the inning's third batter, Dirk Scooter, the Yankee shortstop, he missed with the next three pitches. The count went full.

"Now he's trying to be too fine," said Mark. "He's got to just stick to what he's been doing. Use the buckler to set up the leaflutz and mix in the dipster to keep 'em honest. Right?"

"Right," said Mr. McCord, a fellow season ticket holder, who sat one row behind.

The next pitch was, sure enough, a buckler that sailed in tight. But with two strikes, Scooter had to protect. He swung hard to fight it off and ended up launching a high pop fly straight up the elevator shaft behind third base. Continuing to rise, the white satellite began to tail off toward the stands.

"It's coming our way!" shouted Stats.

Mark already had his glove high in the air.

"Wait!" Stats threw his arm across Mark's chest. "Don't cause interference."

"I won't. But if it's out of play, I'm bringing it in."

As the ball descended, both boys toed the barrier fence to watch.

Then the thunder began.

Not true thunder, exactly, but the next-closest thing. Stats lowered his gaze just in time to see gold-glove shortstop Rico Ruíz, maybe fifteen feet away, pounding the earth, rushing at them both full blast.

"Duck!" Stats covered his head with his forearms and fell to the concrete floor, knocking against Mark, who obviously had the same idea.

The shortstop crashed into the wall. Stats cringed. Then the great Red Sox hero tumbled into the stands, headfirst, his feet somewhere high in the sky. Stats and Mark, hunkered against their folded seats, shared the brunt of the man's fall, pushing Stats one way and Mark the other.

As Stats slid away, he felt his knee snag onto something, then jolt forward. He opened his eyes and slipped his hands from his face. Folded up as he was with his head tucked into his chest, Stats had a perfect view.

First, he saw black leather. Then he saw white.

The ball lay on concrete, trapped under the shortstop's black glove. Right where Stats's knee had knocked it.

The "snag" had been the tip of the shortstop's glove.

Oh, no! thought Stats. *I made him drop it.* All that hustle, all that trouble for nothing!

He closed his eyes, still adrift in the moment's awe. "That was unbelievable."

Those last words went unheard, buried by the roar that erupted next. Why are they cheering? he wondered.

That's when he spotted the veteran Ruíz holding the ball high in the palm of his glove.

A *catch.* He was claiming he'd caught the ball.

Yes! thought Stats. He did. That is, he would've if I hadn't knocked it loose.

But the umpire had been right there, on top of the play. He shook his head, bending at the waist, swinging his arms sideways. In an instant, that "no catch" gesture rolled into a two-palms-up juggling motion showing the crowd that Rico never had full possession of the ball.

That, of course, caused Rico to feign indignity, but the ump, Jim Joyce, was known for his keen eye and accuracy, and the Boston fans soon settled into acceptance.

On the very next pitch, the lucky batter walked. In a bid to get ahead of the Yankees' cleanup hitter, Reggie Marruth, Billee grooved a fastball, and hard-hitting Reggie jacked a rocket into the right-field seats. Two-run homer. In a flash, all of Billee's keen, methodical work had turned into two bad-luck runs. Not insurmountable, but if not for Stats's knee, the game would still be tied, 0–0.

CHAPTER **4**

Billee came out of the game after going seven full innings, with the Sox still trailing 2–0.

That score held until the bottom of the ninth, when Kenny "Hawkeye" Jensen pinch-hit for Drew Evans and singled up the middle, bringing the top of the Red Sox batting order to the plate.

"Hey, Rico's gonna hit this inning," said Mark. "One on, no outs. He's in the hole."

"Unless they get a double play," Stats said quietly. There was something about having caused your home team to lose an out—which then cost them two runs—that saps the optimism from your heart.

The pinch hitter on first gave way to a pinch runner, speed-ster Robertos Davíd, who promptly stole second.

"Tough to double him up now," said Mark.

Stats only watched, willing the batter, Wadell Fens, the Sox's leadoff man, to drive the run in with a clean base hit and get a rally going. The Sox needed more than one run to stay in this game.

Stats took off his hat, turned it inside out, and put it back on.

It seemed the lucky rally cap strategy didn't help much. Fens went after an off-speed pitch and lofted a soft flare to deep short, which Dirk Scooter tracked down. One away. The next guy, Doretta, grounded out to third, freezing the runner at second. Two out.

The Sox were now down to their last hope. Luckily, it was their best hope. Walking in from the on-deck circle came Boston's leading hitter. The crowd was already rising.

"Now batting for the Red Sox," came the rich, resonant voice over the ballpark's loudspeakers, "the shortstop, Rico Ru-íz!"

From the kelly-green girders high above home plate to the thirty-seven-foot Green Monster wall in left field, the elegant ballyard built a century ago shook in the thunderous roll of one long tuba-like drone.

"Ruu-eez!"

No one, however, bellowed with more gusto than Stats and Mark Pagano, who pumped their fists into the warm night sky as Mark's favorite player of all time, Rico "the Breeze" Ruíz, approached the plate.

Hitting an amazing .369 through today, May 12, and representing the tying run, Ruíz slowly, calmly strolled to the dish.

"Here comes an RBI single," Stats announced. "Guaranteed."

"Only a single, Freddy?" yelled Mr. McCord. "I'll bet he parks it."

A retired music teacher, Mr. McCord always brought lucky drumsticks with him. No, not wooden drumsticks, but the frozen ice cream kind, which he and Mrs. McCord passed out for good luck to Mark and Stats and anyone else who sat nearby. And for extra luck, in the middle of the eighth inning, they would hand out Mrs. McCord's freshly baked double fudge brownies, which she called "Sweet Carolines."

Oh, oh, oh. The brownies were so good—and long gone by now.

Mark answered for his kid brother. "Anything, Mr. McCord, anything. We don't care." Mark, who was also a shortstop and was regarded by local coaches as one of South Boston's brightest young stars, idolized the Puerto Rican ballplayer, especially the way Ruíz always seemed to come through in the clutch.

He leaned over. "What do you say, bro?"

Stats pointed to Ruíz's line in his well-worn scorebook.

"He's due. Oh-for-six with a walk, counting last night. Three-for-eleven in the series. He's *over*due."

The first pitch from the Yankees' closer, "Goose Egg" Page, came high and tight, forcing Ruíz to flinch back.

The boos rained down like a June monsoon.

"Whaddya 'fraid of, you rag arm?" came one shout. "Throw the ball o-vah!"

Other fans joined in. "Hey, Page! Show him that inside heat again and your goose egg'll be cooked."

The second pitch fell off, low and away, and the tall, trim left-handed slugger with home-run punch barely moved. Again, a cascade of boos.

"They're pitching around him," said Mark. "Not gonna give him anything to hit."

Stats had already figured that. Even with the cleanup batter on deck, first base was open. Why throw anything decent to the league's best hitter? If he walked, it would at least set up a force play on the bases.

"Playing the percentages," he said, mostly to himself.

Jorgi Berron, the Yankees' catcher, moved his target inside this time, probably hoping that Ruíz, anxious for a key hit, might swing at a pitch in on his fists and pop it up.

Fat chance, thought Stats. Rico was a student of the strike zone.

Instead the nimble lefty with lightning hands got out ahead of an inside slider and drove a rocketing line drive into the right-field corner.

The crowd exploded as the Breeze blew around first base, digging for two, while Davíd jogged home from second with Boston's first run.

But this would be no two-base hit. As the ball smacked against the base of the curvy fence line the old-timers called "the belly," it took a good-luck bounce—straight up. Rico never broke stride, rounding second and digging for third.

Stats stood dumbstruck, his eyes wide, as he took in the grand moment. Running with the precision and balance of a full-tilt motocross biker, Ruíz arced toward deep short, then angled back, driving now on the sides of his shoes and carving out a track toward third.

He did not stop there, though. The relay from deep right was airmailed over the cutoff man, scooting past the shortstop, and bounded all the way to the wall behind third.

In fact, the ball kicked straight up the barrier fence in front of Stats, just beyond the on-field media pit, spinning like a curve ball in front of his nose. It was all he could do to keep from reaching out and grabbing it.

"Go!" he shouted at Ruíz. "Go!"

That's when the strangest thing happened.

From out of nowhere, the pitcher raced up, and, as if the ball had been suspended in midair waiting for him, he grabbed it bare-handed, spun, grunted like a goose, and fired a bullet toward home. The shot flew past Ruíz's shoulder just as he was beginning his dive.

This play would be close. Stats and Mark flung themselves halfway over the fence to get a better view.

Headfirst slide. Catcher's swipe. Flashbulb lights. Stats squinted to take it all in.

Crouched nearby to get the best angle on the bang-bang play, umpire Jim Joyce immediately pointed at the plate and then, in a backlash motion, raised his forearm and fist.

Out at home. Game over. Just like that.

Groans of disbelief shook through the park, rattling the stands like a late-night cargo flight out of Logan.

Stats could not believe it. His stomach tightened. A wave of sadness rolled through him.

He began recalling the scene right away, as much to figure out how to score it as to relive the mad dash toward third and the up-close action that followed. It was a trick he liked to use to postpone feeling crushed by the surprise ending of a come-back attempt cut short. Not to say that it worked. But it was better than nothing.

"That was wicked crazy," said Mark, his voice filled with disbelief. "Woulda been an inside the *parker*."

"He had to go for it," mumbled Stats. "Rounding third, two outs."

"I know. But what a way to lose a game."

"Oh, don't worry," said Mr. McCord. "They've got plenty more ways than that. And I've seen most of them."

Stats bent over his scorebook and began to record the play. He circled the 2B on Ruíz's line, giving him a double, then wrote "E-9" between second and third base, showing Ruíz's advance had come on the right fielder's throwing error. Between third and home, he drew a hash mark, then wrote the number "3" and circled it to indicate Mark's hero had been the third out. Next to that he wrote "1-2," showing that a throw from the pitcher to the catcher had done it. Carefully, he darkened the diamond in Davíd's box to highlight the lone Red Sox run.

Through the process of recording the play, he had preserved it for all time. Almost anyone reading the codes could re-create the play closely enough to understand, more or less, what had happened.

There was no code, however, for a "wicked" hop, a weird spinning ball spookily held aloft just long enough for a gangly, slip-footed pitcher to run under it, grab it, and complete a nearly impossible play.

Nor was there a code for "kid in stands kicks ball out of shortstop's glove."

Stats sat back. Realizing Billee had just lost another one-run game due to sheer bad luck, for which Stats was hugely to blame, he perused his scorebook.

Finally, at the bottom of the page, he added one more entry. Two words. *Curse on*.

CHAPTER 5

The Pagano family home comprised the top half of a two-story brick building located not far from Fenway Park, in a run-down commercial zone on Shawmut, near Lenox. The seventy-five-year-old tall, gray, rectangular structure held not only their modest two-bedroom apartment, but a small neighborhood grocery store below, which Mama Pagano had run up until the time she entered the hospital.

Before climbing the creaky wooden stairway that ran along the exterior of the building, Stats decided to go into the little store.

"Be right up," he told Mark. "I'm gonna grab a box of cereal for the morning."

After removing the key from its hiding place behind a lone red brick lodged nine rows up, Stats unlocked and slowly pushed open the heavy wood-framed glass door. A tiny bell clinked.

It was dark as usual, though a nearby streetlamp shed enough light for him to get around. The place had been dark for over four years, ever since his mother had died. In fact, Stats was just about the only one who'd bothered to enter the store in all that time. Often, he would do it to pick up an item they had run out of in the house above.

Cereal, he had discovered, was one of several products, like certain canned goods and some juices, that kept quite well even years after the expiration date. Stock was, however, running low, so these days Stats only came "shopping" when he absolutely had to.

Of course, he visited for other reasons, too. He had learned some time ago that it was a good way to feel a bit closer to Mama Pagano. In fact, she was almost always there.

"Just grabbing some honey-puffed rice, Mama," he said, passing the first aisle. "Did you hear about the mission Billee and I are on? He thinks there's a new curse. What do you think?"

Stats paused, hoping to sense a response. After a direct question, she would often send a sort of "nudge" or an intuitive feeling to him right away. This time Stats felt nothing strong enough to take as an answer.

He walked on. "Well, if there is, maybe you could give us a few tips on how to stop it."

That sort of request was normal for Stats. He had frequently asked his mother for ideas and help in whatever the family was interested in doing—or struggling to do.

At the cereal aisle, he removed a box. As he returned to the door, he noticed an envelope the postman had slipped through the mail slot. This rarely happened anymore, but sometimes if the letter seemed "official" enough, the post office would deliver it.

Stats debated over whether he should take it upstairs to Pops or leave it, as he normally did, on the dusty pile of mail that had accumulated at the checkout counter over the years.

Pops, you see, was not yet ready to sort things out down here. In fact, Stats and Mark figured it was something they would have to do themselves one day.

Quietly checking in again with his mother, Stats felt a strong urge to compromise, almost as if it were a direct order. He would leave the letter on the counter, but be sure to tell Pops about it—just in case it was important.

"'Night, Mama," he said, pulling the door shut. "See you later."

Awakening the next morning, Stats sat up and swung his legs to the bedside. But he didn't get out of bed. For a moment he watched his brother doing his push-ups. Every day, the same thing. Exercise. Practice. Work hard. From the earliest times Stats could remember, Mark had dreamed of playing shortstop for the Red Sox. Probably lots of guys had that dream. But Stats knew baseball and he knew Mark's stats. He was one guy who actually had a chance.

Mark gasped out, ". . . ninety-eight, ninety-nine, one hundred." Then he collapsed and rolled over.

"What's up, lil' bro?"

Stats felt his heart skip the way it did sometimes when a

valve misfired—or when he thought about something that worried him.

"In the store last night," he started, "I found an important-looking letter. I think I should tell Pops about it."

He fell back down onto his pillow. His heartbeats had slowed to a lazy throb as the pressure increased, then they pounded out a double thump against his middle ribs in a moment of great release. After that, he felt fine.

Mark stood. "You okay, Freddy?"

"Yeah." He looked away as he felt Mark study his face.

"Your heart?"

"No. I mean, a little bit." He hated having anyone make a fuss over him. "I'm okay." And at the moment, that was true.

Mark lingered at his bedside. "If you weren't, you'd tell me, right?"

Stats nodded.

"Okay, then." Mark backed off. "So, listen. Don't worry Pops about any new letters or anything. He's doing better now than ever. We'll get down there one day and go through everything. All right?" He slapped Stats lightly on the jawbone. "Come on, get up. We got a day game at Fenway this afternoon."

While Mark and Pops worked the stand for Sunday's early crowd, Stats headed down to Gate C, near right field, where he figured he could find Bull Brickner, a longtime usher—and a big Papa Pagano's customer—who would let him dash in to do a little more field research for Billee.

"Yeah, hey, bubba," Bull greeted him. "Hop over and come on in."

Being just a bit over four feet tall, it was actually easier for Stats to duck under the turnstile, so he did. "Thanks, Bull. Be right back."

He hustled through the corridors, ending up in the seats behind the Red Sox dugout, trying to spot someone from the grounds crew. Leaning over the short fence near the media pit, he spied Paolo Williams down on the field battling a huge bag of something stuck in a wheelbarrow.

"Hi, Paolo," he called.

The man looked up. "Say there, Freddy Ballgame! How ya doin'? Boy, what about them Sox, huh? Maybe today they avoid the sweep, you think? If we could just get Billee back in the groove, eh? When he's going good, seems like the whole team goes good. And when he's not . . ." He lowered his head, adding a twist.

"Yeah, I know. That's what Billee thinks, too. And I was just wondering, do you think anything about the field, the pitcher's mound, for example, could've been changed recently that might be causing him any trouble?"

Paolo thought a moment. "Nothing I can recall. We replace the sod every year and pack new clay around the mound, but it's exactly the way it was last year when he pitched so good and the years before that, too."

Stats narrowed his eyes and pursed his lips a moment. "Yeah, okay. I was just trying to—"

35

"I'll tell you, son, Billee's just having an off year, that's all it is. Happens to these young pitchers. Happens a lot. Especially after a year of success. Sophomore jinx, they call it."

Stats let his head droop. "Jinx" was just another word for curse. "I thought maybe something about the ballpark might've changed between last year and this year that would explain his bad luck."

"Sorry, Freddy. Nothing I can think of. You might talk to Ol' Red, though. He's been around here longer than any of us, and he runs the show, eh? If anybody had some inside intel for you, it'd be Ol' Red."

"Yeah, right," said Stats. He did not exactly brighten at that idea. Ol' Red would be Chas Herman "Red" Gruffin, park maintenance supervisor and well known to be a grumpy old frankenfurt who never had much more than a scattershot word to say to anybody.

Stats decided he would see how today's game turned out first. Then, if he absolutely needed to, he'd put on his Sherlock Holmes hat—that is, the hood on his Red Sox hoodie—and continue his investigation with grumpy Ol' Red.

CHAPTER 6

For the first time in his life Stats felt uneasy sitting in Fenway Park. The game had just ended. Mercifully. And that was not just because of the lopsided score, 11–3 Yanks. It was a merciful ending because of the merciless way a number of rowdy fans had turned against the hometown team during the last three innings of the romp.

They were so harsh and so enraged. And being so derogatory in front of their fiercest rivals, of all teams!

"My granny could've made that play!" one guy shouted at Drew Evans in right field. "And she can't even go to her left!"

"Johnny Damon could've made that play!" spat another, referring to a former Sox hero with a questionable arm, who later joined the Yankees.

When a sizzler skipped past second baseman Dusty Doretta, another fan, named Lucy, who sat near Stats, squawked, "Nice form, Dusty—if you were a *matador*!"

After the number eight hitter, Burlin Fiske, struck out to end the eighth, Announcer Bouncer yelled, "Hey, Burly! At least you went down swinging—you looked just like Don Zimmer against Pedro!"

That one was just plain cruel. Zimmer was seventy-two years old when he and former Sox ace Pedro Martinez had tangled on the field.

After the game, Stats told Mark he needed to find Billee. "Tomorrow's an off day, and they're leaving town, so it's my last chance."

"Yeah, okay, but don't take too long. I'll get me some fries at Jake's and watch a little NESN."

"I'll meet you there."

Before tracking down Billee, Stats decided to find Ol' Red and ask some quick questions. After a few inquiries, he located Red Gruffin in the "irrigation pit" where all the sprinkler piping, terminals, and control valves were housed. He did not look happy.

"Uh, hello? Mr. Gruffin? Sorry to bother you."

Ol' Red glanced up, bit down on his unlit cigar stump, and spat out a gooey brown chunk into the muddy pit in front of him. He went back to work.

Stats took that as an invitation to leave. He stepped back slowly and turned.

"What the blazes do you want?" growled Red.

The sudden surge to his heart was something Stats did not want, or need, at this moment. He stood frozen, except for the full body shake his heart had started.

"Huh?" the old man hacked out. "You want something? If not, why the devil are you down here bothering me?"

Barely managing to turn back toward the man, Stats wondered if it would be possible to speak with frozen lips and no breath. In any case, he knew he was going to have to find out.

"Um, I'm here to see if, I mean Paolo—Mr. Williams—thought . . ."

"What's that good-for-nothing foul pole Paolo got to do with this?"

Stats released a small amount of the air trapped in his lungs. "He, uh, he just told me . . . that you were the number one expert on . . . on Fenway Park in the whole city."

He squeezed his eyes shut at that desperate attempt to flatter a fire-breathing dragon.

When he reopened them, Mr. Gruffin had turned and was daggering Stats with his own eyes.

"Well, if I am, it's only on account of nobody else around here does their own job worth a damp diddly-squat. Here I am, supervisor, on a Sunday, hunched over, pushing a monkey wrench down in the swamp." He spat again.

"Um, well. I can be real quick."

"Free country."

Stats took another step and hunkered down, not so much to be closer, but in order to let his breathless words approach an audible level.

"Okay, thanks. Um, there's been a lot of—I mean, Billee Orbitt said—"

"Orbitt? That loony goon hasn't got two brain cells to rub together. What's he babbling on about now?"

Stats covered his face with his hands in frustration.

"Okay, okay! Sorry," he blurted out. "I was just wondering if there's been, like, any changes to the park or something that might make things out of balance. That's all!" And that was the best he could do.

Ol' Red appeared somewhat shocked at the outburst. He steadied himself on one knee and took a moment to respond.

"Changes? Cripes, kid, look around. Seats on top of the Green Monster, two new rows of box seats up and down the baselines, cramping the ballfield, making extra work for me and my guys."

Stats had never considered the recent years of remodeling through a groundskeeper's eyes. He only knew that if it weren't for the nearby media pit next to the visitors' dugout, his own seats would now be in row three instead of up front.

"Hold right there." Mr. Gruffin gripped his massive pipe wrench and pulled the handle toward his chest with a grunt. Then he left it hanging in midair while he yanked a rag out of his back pocket to rub the sweat from his neck.

Still squatting, he turned to face Stats. "Outta balance, huh?" He pointed with his cigar to a pile of debris. "Sit down, kid. I'll give you something to chew on, if that's what you want."

Stats made his way to the clump of construction rubble and sat, careful not to step on a soggy cigar stub, in case that was the thing he was going to have to chew on.

"Lessee, now," Ol' Red started. "Place was a pigsty when I hired on, back in the summer of '86. I got in and had everything scoured up spic-and-span-like. Couldn't believe what I saw. Here this outfit was sitting in the catbird seat, heading for the World Series, and the park looked a track-shack mess. But we cleaned her up, top to bottom, good as we could get her."

1986, thought Stats. The year of Game Six. A devastating year, when the Sox came within one out—one strike!—of winning the World Series, and breaking the curse, only to see it dribble away.

Some say that was the year "The Curse" officially entered the vocabulary of Red Sox Nation, though others claim they'd felt it in their bones long before then.

Stats leaned forward. "Anything special stand out to you about that year?"

"Special? Well, other than pumping the tunnels free of muddy groundwater, bleaching out the mold growing everywhere, and flooding out the rats and mice, no, nothing all that special."

Stats entered the info into his eXfyle smartphone, instantly forming a picture in his mind of what that must have looked like. Waterfalls crashing from the upper decks. Rivers rushing down the narrow cement aisles between the rows of wood-slat seats, spilling onto a puddling field.

"That was the one per-dicament, though," Red continued, "I couldn't get a handle on that per-ticular year. Rodents. Still deal with 'em every year. But it got better after the '86 World

41

Series, let's put it that way. I mean, just like any other ballpark in the country, there's gonna be rats. But, looking back, ever since '02 when the new owners started all this remodeling, it's been up one year, down the next. For example, 2003, they added the Green Monster seats. That crazy project ran on longer than they figured, so we never got out ahead of 'em. Same with '06—the .406 Club and that whole mess. All through the season we kept fighting rats. Have to say, 2003 and 2006 were the worst years as far as pests go. All that remodeling."

This *was* a *lot* to chew on, thought Stats. The worst years, as far as critter control, were both heartbreak years.

"Which years seemed like the easiest?"

"Easy? Cripes, kid, never easy." He puzzled on it a moment. "I'd guess '04 was probably better than most. Maybe '07."

Whoa. *The world championship years*. Could there really be a connection? No, he thought, *no way*. He felt pretty silly even considering the idea. He could buy Billee's mystic theory of the park being out of whack, even bad karma. But how could the rodent population have anything to do with a ball team's balance? Even so, he wrote it all down.

"Hey, look, kid. I gotta get back to earning a buck."

"Sure, sorry." Stats rose. "Thanks for your help."

Mr. Gruffin lifted his chin and grunted again, then re-wedged the cigar stub between his teeth.

But before Stats could leave, the crusty old man plucked the stub from his mouth with a pop. "Hey, kid. What'd you say your name was?"

"I, uh, I'm Freddy, but people call me Stats."

"Yeah, okay, Stamps. If I think of anything else, I'll tell that nincompoop Paolo."

"Wow, that'd be great. Thanks!"

For a grumpy old curmudgeon, Ol' Red Gruffin didn't seem all that bad. In fact, he might have just given Stats a big ol' clue.

CHAPTER **7**

Anxious to tell Billee what he'd just learned, Stats journeyed out to the pitcher's favorite postgame retreat, a wooden chair in the shade of the Red Sox bull pen way out in right field.

Stepping through the gate on the first-base side—one priceless perk that came with having grown up in this park—he began his trek across the sacred turf. And to Stats, it always felt like the first time, an instantaneous feeling of having stepped upon a magical green carpet, ready to transport him anywhere in the ballpark's past.

He crossed the infield between first and second and momentarily stood back as Carlton Fisk bounded past the first-base bag in the 1975 World Series after performing an arm-slashing body-English dance to keep a game-winning twelfth-inning foul-line-hugging home run fair. With each step Stats journeyed deeper into the lush meadow of infinite ballgames—the ones that would last forever. Looking up, he saw Big Papi's twelfth-inning walk-off homer sail over the Green Monster in Game 4 of the 2004 play-offs against the Yankees. That one never came down—and it turned The Curse around.

Beneath him, the well-seasoned Kentucky bluegrass, thick with memories, caught each footfall, softly, gently. The earth below seemed to possess its own heartbeat, strong and healthy. And the more he walked, the more the ballpark's heart meshed with his own.

This place was his sanctuary, his safe spot, his home, where it was always summertime and the breathing was easy.

"Hey, Billee," he called toward the lonesome figure shrouded in white. "Tough game, huh?"

"They hate to see us lose, don't they?" the pitcher said through his cotton towel wrap.

"I guess so."

"Any news?"

"Well, maybe." Stats allowed Billee time to unravel the long white cloth covering his face and head before he began. "Red Gruffin told me that pretty much the only years he could re-member, going back to when he got here in 1986, that he didn't have to battle a bunch of rats and mice were 2004 and 2007."

Billee let the towel drape down around his neck, then gripped each side. He stood up and took a few paces. A pained look clouded his face as he studied the sky. "What the heck would rats and mice have to do with anything?"

"Well, I don't know, but it—"

Billee cut him off with a raised hand. His steel-gray eyes panned the ballpark, from the first-base seats to the center-field nook, as if he were letting this newly proffered rodential concept and all of its ramifications sink in.

"During '04 and '07, huh?" he said. "And the Sox haven't been near a World Series since."

"Right. And check this out. The worst years for rodents were '03 and '06." After a moment, he added, "Do you think there's a connection?"

Billee spun toward him. "There's always a connection. But what it is, I don't know." Pacing one way, then back the other, Billee launched into a rundown on the current team.

"Today, Sammy Jethroe said his timing at the plate has never been better, but nothing falls in. Wadell Fens has lined into three double plays with runners in scoring position. Not to mention the rotten luck Teddy Lynn and Dusty are having. Who's next?"

Billee walked to the bull pen fence and leaned on it. "I know it's only the middle of May, but Rico says he already sent off to his *tía* Blanca back home for some sort of pepper, rum, sheep's fat, and cactus-apple concoction to marinate his bats in to bring back the power. Cedro Marichal sleeps with sliced green Dominican papayas wrapped around his pitching arm to help coax back his holy ghost pitch—the one no batter can see. Each day, another guy goes down. And no one knows how to break us out of it. I just wish I could do *something*. But what?"

Billee scanned the ballpark once again. "It's not the first time, though, is it? These curses go way back. Oh, if these walls could talk."

Hearing Billee's befuddlement caused Stats to gaze off in equal discomfort. He was about to suggest a retreat into logic, a sort of "cooling off" period, wherein curse talk was put on hold for a while—at least until they found out if the cactus-apple-rum marinade showed any promise. But before he could, Billee brought a finger to his lips and tilted his head, as if listening for a talking wall.

Stats froze too. It was obviously a weird notion, though not any zanier than connecting rats to curses or bats to cactus, but if these walls *were* going to speak, he didn't want to miss a word.

The silence went on for a minute or so, a long enough time for Stats to feel fully self-conscious, if not a bit silly. He was about to say something when, from high in the sky, there came an eerie screech.

"Chee! Chee!"

A lone hawk circled above the infield, orbiting counterclockwise, as if running the bases backward.

Continuing its graceful glide, the bird screamed again, this time, it seemed to Stats, with more purpose.

"K'chee! K'chee!" Then it flapped its wings and broke out of its wheeling sail, rising up above home plate, over the top of the announcers' booth facade, and out of sight.

"Whoa," said Billee, speaking in a hushed tone. "That was weird."

Stats was actually feeling a bit strange about it, too, but upon hearing that pronouncement come from Billee, the event now took on an even grander sense of woo-hooery.

Shivers rippled his spare and bony frame.

Billee held his skyward glare. "Well, we got our wish, bud. The walls just talked."

"They did?"

"Yep," said Billee. "No doubt. Got just what we asked for. Alls I wish now is that I knew what they said."

Stats had no clue, either. Statistics he could handle. Astronomy he could handle. Even global geometry. But his personal contact with the great outdoors stopped at the edges of his roof where his telescope sat. And from there he could not ever recall seeing a hawk. Or hearing one talk.

"So what do we do now?" he asked.

"Early this morning," said Billee, still facing the ballfield, "I was so shook up, I drove out to Walden Pond, just to hike around the place, watch the sun rise, meditate. That lake and the woods out there, it always calms me down after a tough game. Anyhow, at the break of day, I remembered what Dr. John Mack, a Harvard professor, once said. 'You have to consider everything.' He said that's the error our scientists make. They set limits on what they'll explore. Because when you set limits, Dr. Mack said, you miss exploring the things that really matter."

He looked at Stats. "So, kid, rats and mice? Might just be exactly what we need to look at. Talking hawks? Why not? I'll tell you one thing. There is so much we don't know. And there's only so much we can ever know. We might as well find out everything we can."

Billee turned and began to walk back to the bull pen. He waved his hand. "Go. Do your thing, Stat Man. I gotta crawl back inside the pen, pull a towel around my head, and meditate."

CHAPTER 8

Stats and Mark arrived at home that Sunday evening around dinnertime. As soon as he entered, Stats felt a sense of something being amiss. The curtains were pulled. The house lights dimmed. And nothing was cooking. Walking inside, they spied Pops sitting in a chair by the bay window, gazing out.

"Markangelo," he said without bothering to look. "You and Alfredo, come to me over here."

The very tone of his words worried Stats and started his heart thumping. He and Mark gathered together in the alcove behind their father as he continued to stare through the lace curtains facing the street.

"You know, boys, I always try to do what's right. But sometimes . . ." He lowered his elbows to the table and prayerfully clutched both hands together.

"Sometimes what, Pops?" said Mark.

Pops had trouble speaking, which only increased the sense of panic washing over Stats.

Finally he said, "I sometimes—I let little details slip away from me. I knew this day was bound to come. I hate thinking how I put it off for so long. Now I got myself in a tight spot."

Pops reached out across the table and picked up an envelope. Stats recognized it immediately as being the one he'd seen downstairs the night before. He had followed Mark's advice not to tell Pops about it, even though he'd told his mother he would. Somehow, though, Pops had received the message. He withdrew the letter from inside.

"This," he said, "is from a bill collector. It has to do with your mother's store. They say we still owe them money."

Okay, thought Stats, feeling somewhat relieved. It's a money problem. It's not life or death, it's not a brain tumor. He's not running off and joining a kung fu academy in China—something Stats had always imagined *he* might do if he were ever in big enough trouble.

"How much is it for?" asked Mark.

Good question. The sooner Stats got a number, the sooner he could start working on a solution.

"We can help," Stats added. "We've got money saved up." The tip jar at the stand was always split between them, and it garnered as much as sixty dollars a day.

"No, no, you boys—"

"Pops, let us help," said Mark. "We're all in this together. We're part of the family business, too."

Pops drew in a slow breath, scanning their faces, although the depth of his focus seemed far away.

"Alfredo, Markangelo. Back when your mother was sick . . ." He finger-painted a tiny cross over his heart. "I had so many things on my mind." He held his hands out as if they were paddles, and as he spoke, he knocked each phrase between them. "The baseball season was starting up, you boys were in two different schools, we had medical bills and all of that. I could barely pay my own vendors, let alone what had piled up on the store." He stopped to take a weary sigh. "And after she passed . . ."

He stopped again, dropping his chin to his chest, wrapping his thick arms around himself, and he shook.

It was a lot for Stats to take in. Pops had rarely spoken about Mama in the four years since her death. But Stats did know his mother had been the money-minder.

He watched his father, a bear of a man, now bent forward, his fingertips pressed against the gray of his temples.

"I knew we had some debts to clear up. I just never dreamed . . ."

"It's okay, Pops," said Mark, taking his father's shoulder into his palm. "We'll get through this. Don't worry about anything. But, just—how much is it?"

Pops puffed out a burst of wind and shook his jowls. "Too much. More than I have." He looked off across the street again. "I always hoped I could, someday, save up a little seed money to help produce my inventions, but now . . ."

The inventions Pops spoke of were culinary. He was always experimenting with new recipes for hot dogs and buns, especially during the off-season. Most importantly, he had tried for years to perfect the skin of his veggie dogs so they would blister up and pop when he grilled them—the way the skins on regular hot dogs did. However, the idea that Pops dreamed about saving up seed money to put the recipes into production was a new concept to Stats.

"And these people," Pops went on, "they can cause real trouble. They can hound you day and night. They can come knock on your door at any time, bring in a U.S. marshal, and take everything." He sent another look out across Shamut Ave. "It's just that, you boys should know."

"Pops," said Mark, "please tell me how much it is. How much do we owe?"

Pops handed him the letter.

Stats leaned over Mark's shoulder to read along. The page was stamped in red: THIRD AND FINAL NOTICE! It showed account after account from four years ago and a grand total. It showed another amount for interest and lawyers' fees. The final number was easy to find, typed out boldface, in both numerals and words. The agency claimed that, in total, Pops owed them *One Hundred Thirty-one Thousand Nine Hundred Fifty-five Dollars*.

Stats mouthed a soft "Ho-oh." He looked at Mark.

Mark clamped his jaw tight and stood rigid.

Someone banged on the door.

CHAPTER 9

Everyone turned and stared at the dark blue door.

Mark took a step. "I'll get it."

"Wait," said Stats, casting uncertain eyes at Pops.

"No, no, it's okay." Pops raised his hand. "Answer the door." He stood, seeming ready to face whatever was waiting for him on the top landing outside.

Mark walked over and grasped the handle, then cracked the door open.

"Hit me with your best shot, Marko!"

On the porch stood the one and only Billee Orbitt.

"Hey, Billee." Mark reached out and slapped the pitcher's flattened palm. "What are you doing here?"

"I was just heading home, so I thought I'd stop by." He peeked in. "Hey, Stat Man. Hiya, Pops."

Now standing at the head of the dining room table, Pops sent a big smile, as if his mood had been instantly transformed. "Good to see you, Billee. Come on in. Can I get you something to drink? Something to eat?"

"Thanks. Iced tea, maybe? You make the best there is."

"Coming right up." Pops shook a finger as he answered and retreated to the kitchen.

Just seeing his father's finger stab, that small confident gesture, sent a wave of calm through Stats.

"Look," said Billee. "I was on my way down to Merry Mount when an idea hit me, and I wanted to talk to Stats about it."

"Me?" Stats wandered out of the alcove to meet Billee at the table. "Sure."

Billee gave Stats a wink, then pulled out a chair. They both sat.

"Okay, here's what I think's going on."

"Going on?" asked Mark, taking a chair across the table to join them.

"Yeah," said Stats. "With the Sox. Listen to this." He sent a head jab toward Billee, as if coolly coordinating a top-secret disclosure.

Billee placed his muscular forearms on the table and leaned forward.

"Marko, I believe there is a brand-new curse upon us. But it's tricky. It's subtle. It's not one everybody's gonna believe in right off."

"Well, I don't," said Mark. "You guys are only three games out. And the season's only six weeks old."

"Yeah, sure," said Billee. "A curse doesn't waste its time on a cellar dweller. Like Shakespeare said, 'When you ain't got nothing, you got nothing to lose.' But when you lose the Wild

Card spot on the last day of a roller-coaster season or lose the clincher game of a World Series, that's when you know you've been served. And I think, just like last year, we're being set up to take a tumble."

"Well, I've seen it happen way too many times," said Pops, returning with a tall glass of tea with a slice of lime floating in it, as well as one of his "experimental" rolls. He set them in front of Billee.

"Thank you, sir." Billee took the glass, then turned to Stats and Mark. "And there's always a pitcher coming off a great year in the thick of it. Look up Mike Torrez or Calvin Schiraldi or Bob Stanley. Right, Pops?"

At hearing the names, Pops closed his eyes and made the sign of the cross.

Stats didn't have to look anything up. He knew all about the pop fly home run Bucky Dent hit for the Yankees in 1978 off Torrez, after a wrenching up-and-down season, to clinch the American League pennant. And the wild pitch Stanley threw in the '86 World Series, to set the stage for the Mets' victory. Who didn't? But he had never considered that curses revolved around pitchers. He then realized, when the Red Sox sold Babe Ruth in 1919, starting *The Curse*, the Babe had been, up to that point, a great pitcher.

"That's what I like about you, Billee," said Pops, tapping his temple. "Always thinking. Baseball's a thinking man's game. Talent only gets you so far. I try to tell that to my Markangelo." He raised a palm toward the ceiling.

"What?" said Mark in protest. "I think. I'm always thinking. It's just that sometimes I think I should stop thinking. Right, Billee?" He knuckled the pitcher's arm.

"You ain't wrong," Billee answered, with a wide grin. "Thinking can go both ways."

Mark grinned, too, looking satisfied.

"Billee," said Pops, with a quick gesture to indicate the handcrafted hollowed-out bread roll in front of him. "Try my latest. See what you think."

Another one of Pops's pet projects was to settle upon a recipe and design for the perfect customized hot dog bun—mainly for Chili Billees, which always seemed to leak.

Billee took a bite. He chewed and smiled broadly.

"Mmm, Pops, I think you might have it right here. Tastes great."

"And more filling!" said Pops. "See how wide the opening is? I can get loads of chili into this one." He gleamed in satisfaction and took a seat.

"Sure can," Billee agreed, still nodding. He then went on with his mission. "Okay now, Stats, tell me this. Have you ever heard of the butterfly effect?"

"I think so."

Mark jumped in. "I have, for sure."

That brought quick looks from Stats and Pops.

"But," said Mark, drumming his fingertips, "I forget what it is. Something about butterflies . . ."

Stats slid his eXfyle close and began typing the words into the search window.

"Don't bother," said Billee. "I'll tell you. The theory is, a butterfly can flap its wings and set off a long chain of events that will affect weather systems to such an extent that a single wing flap can eventually cause a hurricane clear across the globe."

After scanning the entry on his screen, Stats said, "Oh, yeah, the interconnectedness of everything." He looked up. "Ray Bradbury's idea. Yeah, okay . . ." Still reading, he added, "And string theory branches off of it. Yeah, I know a little bit about that."

Mark turned quickly. "You do?"

"Well, it comes from science fiction, mostly time travel stories, where a guy goes back into the past and even if he only changes one tiny thing, that act causes the whole future to morph—since, you know, everything's connected."

Mark sat wide-eyed, stunned.

"Pops," said Billee, "the kid's got a brain in there, I'll tell you."

"And I'll tell you," said Pops, "he didn't get it from me." They both laughed.

Stats got back on point. "So, Billee, what are you saying about the butterfly effect?"

"Basically that a curse is a chain reaction that might be caused by the tiniest thing. So instead of looking around at all the latest construction or all the years of rat problems, maybe we only need to go back and undo one little butterfly flap."

"You lost me, big-time," said Mark.

Stats thought he might have followed Billee's statement well enough, but pressed for clarification. "You mean we need to find the source of the imbalance, right? Like whatever butterfly flap of the wings sort of thing started the first bit of bad luck?"

"Exactamundo," said Billee. "But here's what hit me as I was driving home." He leaned in close. "Maybe it's not a butterfly we're looking for. Maybe it's a hawk."

CHAPTER 10

A normal boy would have, at this point, simply smiled, nodded in agreement, and dismissed everything he had just heard as the mind-bouncings of a spaceman.

Was that all Billee had? Find the tiny cause of this monumental imbalance? Some sort of a hawk wing flap? And then, undo it?

But Stats, of course, was not a normal boy. In fact, he had never aspired to be one. Sure, he wished he could play baseball at least once in his life, the way normal boys of normal height and weight so often do. But he would never trade his love of numbers, his world of complex calculations, his joy of puzzling out solutions to multifarious mysteries for anything. That is, not for anything normal.

And so, even though he figured the chances of fulfilling Billee's request were somewhere between slim and none—and slim had long ago left the ballpark—Stats merely filed away the challenge, then turned to Mark and Pops and let them in on what Billee was talking about.

"A hawk flew around and screeched at us today. We think it might have been giving us a message connected to this new curse."

Mark did his best at stifling an automatic laugh, and was at least able to keep it to a muffled squeak.

The concept, however, did not faze Pops at all.

"A hawk, eh?" he said. "Now, that's possible. My father, may he rest in providence, always told me the same story whenever we saw a hawk. One that goes back to the old country."

"He means Italy," said Mark.

Billee thrust his chin in Mark's direction.

"Papa claimed that whatever thought you're thinking when a hawk appears in your life is one you better pay attention to. A hawk brings resolution." He shaped his fingers into a claw. "'Grab it now,' he's saying."

Then Pops straightened and shrugged, lifting both palms high. "I don't know. That's what he always told me, anyway, and I never forgot it."

"Did it ever work for you?" asked Mark. "Did you ever do something you were thinking of when a hawk flew by?"

"Only one time that I can say for sure. Right after your mother and I got married, we were driving home from out in Sudbury, where she used to live, and she just happened to wonder out loud whether or not she should start her little grocery store."

Pops smiled. But he did not speak, not for quite a while. Soon all eyes left him and his pinched mouth and focused on the table.

In a moment, Pops regrouped. "So right then and there," he continued, his words full of breath, "a hawk flies straight across the roadway in front of us."

A big laugh now *and* the smile. "What could I say to her?" he could barely say through a hoarse laugh. Again, his hands flew up shoulder high, now signaling surrender.

"You followed your heart," said Billee, to the rescue. "You both did. You followed through and opened her store, which is exactly what I would've done."

"Me too," said Mark.

Stats hummed softly in agreement, keeping his eyes below the brim of his cap.

Pops reached out, gathering Billee's empty glass and plate into his hands, and rose. "Anything else?"

"No, no, all set. Thanks."

Pops trundled off into the kitchen.

Billee tapped the table with his fingernails, digesting the moment. As though by brotherly instinct, he then lifted Stats's cap and reset it on his head.

"You need to grow your hair out, Stat Man. So your hat'll fit right."

Stats knew how he looked. He'd ordered the smallest size cap available, but it was still too big. And since it was professional style, it was not adjustable. Thus, when he snugged it down the way he liked it, to where he could feel his lucky Ted Williams all-star card against his skull, it did tend to make his ears fold over, much like a puppy dog's.

Truthfully, he didn't care. He preferred his hair short. One day, he figured, his head would fit the hat—or else, he could just stack a few more baseball cards inside. Besides, as the photo on the card of his current co-occupant showed, the Splendid Splinter's uniform had hung a little loose on him, too, at first.

"When I was a kid," Billee went on, "my curly hair was so wild, my dad wanted me to get it buzzed completely off. But my mom loved it. So there was always a big scene every time I got a haircut. It was like Samson and Goliath."

Everyone laughed, though the reference didn't quite make sense to Stats.

Billee wagged his head. Then, spotting Pops returning to the room, he added, "But like Shakespeare said, 'Hair today, gone tomorrow.' Right, Pops?"

"Hey, watch it, there!" Pops, whose once-dark curly locks were now mostly reduced to a global fringe, sent Billee a stern glare from the table side. But he could not hold it, as a burst of laughter again rocked the room.

Stats enjoyed the feeling and silently sent up a prayer that Billee would always be a member of this clan. Then he returned to the matter at hand.

"What were we thinking, Billee, when we saw the hawk? Do you remember?"

Billee perused the plaster ceiling overhead. "Weren't we thinking about a connection between mice and rats and a bad-luck streak?"

"Oh, yeah. Do you think that confirms a connection?"

"Now more than ever."

"Hmm," said Mark, as if he were preparing to add something. But that was, in fact, all he said.

Billee gave him a nod, then sat back.

"Marko," he asked, "how's your season going?"

"Okay." He brightened. Baseball was in Mark's blood. It was all he dreamed about, though he seldom said so out loud.

"Better'n okay," said Stats. "Ever since we put up a batting cage on the roof, he's been hammering the ball."

"A batting cage? You're kidding. Who pitches?"

"I do," said Stats. "Well, actually I stand behind an old mattress we propped up and toss the ball like a hand grenade. Then I duck."

"That's exactly how I learned to pitch," Billee said, giving Stats a soft poke on the arm. "Can I see it?"

Both Stats and Mark jumped up and headed for the door to the back veranda, where the roof ladder was attached.

Billee followed them outside. His trip up the vertical metal ladder, though, seemed to be a strain. Not physically, but mentally. He kept his jaw clenched and his silvery eyes focused in front of him the whole way, slowly ascending one rung at a time. Once he climbed over the short parapet wall and his foot touched the flat asphalt roof, he relaxed.

He smiled.

Neither boy said a word. Stats figured Billee's caution had something to do with his balance—which had, as he well knew, been off lately. He spun around and opened the door to the chicken-wired wood-framed batting cage, which was wrapped in a second layer of black netting.

Billee walked forward and surveyed the homemade cage, which Stats now realized looked precisely the way one would expect such an enclosure, built out of scavenged neighborhood scraps, baling wire, and duct tape, to look.

"Beautiful," the pitcher said. "Amazing."

Billee appreciated creativity. Stats knew that from last season, after he designed a customized baseball card just for Billee.

Most cards list career stats as well as personal info, such as whether a player bats or throws left handed or right. On the card he handed to Billee during one of the first few times he'd stopped by Papa Pagano's, Stats listed the following:

Billee "Spacecase" Orbitt
HEIGHT: of fashion
WEIGHT: for a better pitch
BORN: to be wild
THROWS: Lefty
BATS: Belfry

It cracked Billee up so much, he caused a minor laugh riot at the stand, reading it off to everyone in line. From then on, it was as if Stats had inherited a best friend. Even Mark had said so, without a speck of jealousy.

Billee studied the batting cage a bit longer, then pushed back from the frame and stepped over to a dried-out, once-blue kitchen chair parked nearby. He took a seat.

"You guys ever come up here at night and just look at the stars?"

"All the time," said Stats. "Well, *I* do."

"Me," said Mark, "not so much. I have a life."

In his own defense Stats added, "He comes up when we spend the night. I bring my telescope, and he looks, too."

"Good on you both. Like Einstein always said, 'Never lose touch with nature. It ain't natural.'"

"When did he say that?" asked Stats.

"Well, words to that effect. Basically, stay connected to the balance of nature. Honor it. No matter if you're a hitter or a pitcher or a whole ball club. Balance is vital. That's what Einstein meant."

So now Billee's interpreting Einstein, thought Stats, amused at the concept, though he could not quibble with the conclusion. Billee was, in his own way, a genius as well.

The pitcher folded his arms and tipped the chair back on its hind legs. "It's all balance. The whole world revolves around balance. Without it, the earth would wobble, right, Stat Man?"

"Well, it actually does anyway."

"See? Lack of balance. It affects everything. Imagine I'm a tightrope walker, and I have you guys balanced on my shoulders, and we're crossing the street from here, say, to Sam Alone's bar over there. If any one of us lost his balance, we'd all be asphalt."

He pointed to both boys. "Why? Because we're all connected."

"Yeah," said Mark. "I saw that happen once on ESPN with a bunch of cheerleaders in a pyramid. Someone in the middle lost it and, dude, legs and other assorted body parts were flying everywhere." Mark shook his head. "Cheerleaders are nuts."

He walked over and picked up one of his bats lying next to the cage. He stepped in. "Billee, throw me a few?"

"Uh, yeah," said Billee, "just a few. Getting dark."

Eyeing Stats, he said, "What do you like to look at up here?"

"Everything. Planets, stars. Constellations. Especially Orion and Pleiades, the Seven Sisters. But my favorite is Pegasus, the Flying Horse. It's right in the middle this month."

"Pegasus is my favorite, too!" said Billee. He held out his hand. "Gimme skin, buddy." They slapped palms.

Billee looked into the dusk. "I remember as a kid looking up at night, waiting for the Flying Horse to rise. My whole life, I've always felt like I was some guy who just got dropped off on this planet one day by mistake, that I didn't really belong. And I always pretended Pegasus was my rescue ship." He smiled into the sky, then lowered his gaze. "Someday, huh, bud?"

Stats grinned and nodded. His heart fluttered. To ride off someday on a flying horse? What an idea.

As Billee stepped into the batting cage, he added, "Once I get back from out of town, I'll help you sort things out. Okay, Stat Man? It's a long trip. Ten days, then we're home for six. So dig up anything you can. About hawks, about rats, wing flaps, energy vibes, and maybe dig up a few quahogs, if you got the time." He winked.

Stats beamed. Being a clam chowder fanatic, the mere image of going out quahog digging along Ipswich Bay with his four-pronged clam rake at least gave him a starting point.

Plus, it provided another point to ponder. Would a clam closing up its shell count as a wing flap?

CHAPTER **11**

Stats spent the rest of the evening looking into the natural history aspects of ancient New England. Fenway Park, he found out, was built on ancient swampland. "Fen," in fact, stemmed from a Celtic word for "bog," or swamp. And millions of years before that, ancient underground pressures caused huge veins of quartz and amethyst crystals to form all throughout the region. Interestingly enough, quartz crystals actually radiate energy. Healing energy, according to some websites. He typed it all down for Billee's sake. After all, his task was to "dig up anything." However, how any of that information could help him identify the wing flap of a new curse was pure bogglement at the moment.

That night, Stats fell into a fitful sleep. It might have been the excitement of this new assignment from Billee. Maybe it was this new aura of sadness triggered by the unexplainable downward spiral of the Red Sox and the negativity surrounding it. It might even have been worry over the huge debt Pops faced.

67

At any rate, when he awoke later on, the night air seemed so hot and thick, he had trouble catching his breath. At one point he threw off his bedcovers, but even then he felt as if he were lying in a puddle of sweat.

He fumbled for his inhaler and took a shot, but it only provided momentary relief. After a while, he slipped off again into another light and restless doze, all the while trying to ignore the most likely culprit—namely, a series of nerves that had been damaged by a severe fever Stats contracted when he was only two.

The vagus nerve system, which runs from the base of the brain, through the neck, past the heart, lungs, liver, and into the gut, affects your whole life. "Vagus" comes from Latin, meaning "wanderer." And if your wandering or "vagabond" nerve is altered, as was Stats's, it can impact everything from talking (it sparks the tongue) to blood pressure (it sparks the heart) to digestion. For when the vagus nervous system balks, signals get dropped. It's like the faulty wire that causes a lightbulb to blink when it should burn steady. You stutter, your brain clouds up, your heartbeat slows to a crawl, and you can sweat up a storm.

Sometimes, the lights go out.

That's when you faint and fall to the ground, which is no way to wander. Stats—and the poor heart he traveled with—had done it all.

Upon awakening sometime later, he felt as if all the air had vanished from the room. It felt as if he were underwater, deep down, at the bottom of a black lake.

He fought to pull in a breath. He kicked and swam as hard as he could to reach the glinting light at the surface. Finally his mouth popped open and air rushed in. The night sky spiraled above. And then it was over.

He was awake, drawing in huge wheezy breaths, and feeling as though he were on fire.

"Mark," he said between gasps.

"Yeah?" Mark's voice sounded surprisingly clear.

"I'm having . . . trouble . . . breathing."

"I know. I was listening."

Stats could hear his brother sit up.

"What do you need, Freddy? Your inhaler?"

"No, I—Not . . . doing any good."

"Want me to prop your feet up?" That was one tactic to help the heart pump easier. "What can I do?"

For some reason, merely hearing his older brother ask those questions, using his most delicate and reassuring tone, made Stats's eyes well up. Before he could answer, though, his throat closed again. He lay against his pillow, taking in short, quick puffs of air, and wept.

Mark bounced off the bed and stuffed his pillow under Stats's ankles, then dashed out of the room.

In a few moments, Pops knelt at the bedside, holding Stats by his thin, moist wrist. The wide-eyed look that quaked across his father's face was enough to make Stats work as hard as possible to breathe normally. He turned his head to the side to help open his throat and coughed.

It seemed like peanut butter was chugging through his heart, the beats came so slowly.

"Here," said Mark, handing something to Pops. "It's nine-one-one."

It was the last thing Stats would hear that night that made any sense.

CHAPTER 12

Stats heard no sirens, no boot soles bounding up the stairs. His first sensation of the events surrounding his drifting in and out of consciousness was being thrust out into the cool night air, flashing red lights hitting the double-decker wall of the house, and a group of men maneuvering him down the stairway on a wheeled stretcher.

The hiss of oxygen filled his ears as the gas funneled into a clear rubber mask, streaming its way up his nose, down his throat, and into his lungs.

The men talked to each other in firm gruff bursts. He did not remember an ambulance ride. He could not remember hearing the familiar *swack* of the sliding glass doors as he entered the hospital or the room's electric hum. He remembered a falling star.

He saw tall glowing angels in white gowns gliding about. One became a doctor, one a nurse, another an ice cream man, or so it seemed.

At a certain point he woke up out of a dead sleep inside a dimly lit hospital room amid an array of small green, red, and blue lights. Oxygen tubing ran into his nose. Another tube had been taped to his arm, leading to a clear glass bottle that dangled above his bed. It was a familiar environment, and he lay in it awhile, alone, enjoying the ease of breathing. A few moments later he heard a familiar voice.

"Hey, Stat Man. Got here quick as I could."

Billee? Here? That was crazy. How did *he* know?

"Who, uh, who called you?" Stats asked.

"One of the night nurses. Everyone knows me down here, from all the fund-raisers. They said you were asking for me."

"I was?" He lay motionless, looking at the ceiling, which had suddenly brightened.

He heard Billee scoot a chair toward the bed. "How you feeling, big guy?"

"Fine. I still don't—everything seems weird. Is my dad here?"

He tried to lift his head from the pillow, but it made the room swirl. He settled back down.

Billee leaned close. "Your pop's down the hall with Mark, resting. Want me to go get them?"

"No, that's okay. Let them sleep."

"All right." Billee turned his head slightly to eye the doorway behind him, in the same indirect way he might check a base runner on second. Turning back, he said, "I gotta tell you what I found out. Man, it was so obvious, I should've figured it out sooner."

"What out?"

"A long time ago, the ancient Chinese discovered a life-force energy that flows through everything on earth."

"Really?"

"It's what connects us to everything else. It's like the wind, only it can pass right through a mountain."

"Okay." Stats decided he could go along with that.

"This energy has a certain positive feel to it, a certain upbeat rhythm, you could say, like the way good music makes you feel. Anyway, the Chinese found out that when it gets disrupted, bad things happen."

Stats had trouble imagining that. "If it passes right through everything, how can it be disrupted?"

"Great question. The only thing that can affect energy is energy, right?"

Stats had never given the concept much thought, but in his present condition, it seemed to make sense. "I guess."

"Okay, take music. If the musicians play out of tune or a singer sings off-key, it ruins the song, right? Same thing with what the Chinese call your life-force energy. If the harmony is disrupted, by negative off-key energy, let's say, that's when bad things happen."

"I got it," said Stats. "Makes sense."

"Right on. And now the big news. Just before I came here, I had a dream."

Billee held both palms toward Stats as if framing the scene. "I'm floating in the air, high above Fenway Park. But below me, the land is filled with all this bulrush and swamp grass and these ponds of water. The ballfield was there, I could see it, chalk lines and all, but everything was underwater. So instead of the field being some manicured lawn, it was this boggy swamp. And out in the middle of center field there was this huge oak tree. And way up in the tree I see a bird's nest built out of all these long leaves of grass and foxtails and twigs."

"A hawk's nest?"

"That's what I figured, but it was empty. So I turn around and I see the modern-day press box we have right now, full of tall windows, high above home plate, with that metal catwalk running along the base of the glass."

"Okay."

"But then I look closer and I see a red-tailed hawk sitting on the edge of the catwalk. But no nest. And then this huge dark cloud rises up above me." He waved his arms in a slow circle. "Casts a shadow over everything. Then when I look back down, the hawk is gone. Vanished. Nothing. That's when I woke up."

Billee sat back with his hands on his knees. "So now I know what the walls said to us. Through the hawk."

"You do? Out of *that* dream?" No way did Stats see a connection. "What?"

Billy brought his hands to his mouth in the shape of a narrow cup and softly called, "Chee. Chee."

Stats slumped. "Ha ha. Yeah, right, I heard that, too."

"No, but wait. Here's how it all ties in." He leaned even closer. "Guess what the ancient Chinese word happens to be for that special life-force energy."

Stats stared into Billee's misty gray eyes. Did he really think Stats would be able to answer that? He made the only guess he could. "Chee?"

"Exactamundo, Stat Man. You got it. It's spelled 'c-h-i' or sometimes 'q-i.' But it's pronounced 'chee.'"

"Really?" Stats stared into the ceiling tiles as he processed all this new information. He closed his eyes. He saw lightning cut across the Fenway sky.

"I used to take tai chi classes," Billee continued. "To help my focus. That's what made me think of it."

"Mark did, too," said Stats, remembering where he'd heard that term before. "So what does it all mean?"

"Well, for one thing, it means we have to keep our energies focused. The ballpark *is* out of whack. And once we find out why, all we gotta do is whack it back in."

Oh, thought Stats. Is that all?

Billee shuffled in his seat. Stats took a moment to focus his energy, then wiggled onto his side. He opened his eyes.

The room was dark.

CHAPTER 13

Stats caught a little more dreamless sleep before two nurses came in to check on him, double-check the oxygen tubes, and offer a meager breakfast.

"You have a visitor," said one.

In walked Mark, smiling, full of energy. "How's it going, Freddy? Doc says you're gonna live. How'd you sleep?"

"Fine. Sort of. Did you know Billee was here?"

"Billee Orbitt?"

Stats nodded. "A couple of hours ago."

Mark shook his head. "Not likely. It's only six thirty in the morning. You must've been dreaming."

Still feeling a bit groggy, Stats offered no protest. "Where's Pops?"

"Coming. He's getting coffee."

Mark pulled the blackout curtains open, and sunlight exploded all around. "There, that's better." He turned. "Holy cheese, Freddy, you look like you dove headfirst into home plate."

"I do?"

"Don't worry. Doc Roberts said you're gonna be all right. Rough night, that's all. Said they have to do some tests."

"I know I'd feel a lot better if the Sox started winning again. I hate it when they get swept by the Yanks. Did they say when I get to go home?"

"I think you're staying one more night."

"Oh, man. Look at that little TV."

Mark glanced up. "Gonna have to do. Doc Roberts also said your heart rate was down to thirty-three beats per minute."

"Yeah, well," he answered slowly. "Tell the doctor I'm saving them up for later."

"Always calculating something, aren't you, bro?"

Stats grinned. "My all-time record is thirty-one."

"Yeah, well, try not to break that one anytime soon." Mark looked around. "You gonna eat your oatmeal?"

Stats gave the white bowl a quick look. "It's got raisins."

"Can I have it?"

"Sure."

A moment later, Pops came charging into the room juggling three sweet rolls, two cups of juice, and a hot coffee. "Sorry I took so long. First the insurance papers all over again, since our plan changed from last time. Then I saw the doctor in the hall, so I grabbed him. And then I thought you boys might be hungry."

Stats had never seen Pops act so nervous.

"Doc Roberts says you're doing fine. You feel fine?"

"I would if I didn't have all these tubes and wires all over me."

Pops shook his head. "They gotta stay. Your oxygen level was down to eighty-one percent last night. They're not taking any chances."

"So when do I go home?"

Pops looked away as if avoiding Stats's eyes. "Doc's gonna see. Everything's, you know, step-by-step. That's how it's gotta go. He's waiting on the first tests to find out if he has to run some more."

"Oh, man."

Mark tried to help. "What're you complaining about, Freddy? You know how hot your nurse is? I think I might check in just for a sponge bath."

Stats cracked up. It felt good to laugh. That is, until he coughed.

Pops glared at Mark. "Hey, hey, don't get fresh. You're not in the dugout here. Show some manners."

Mark grinned sheepishly. "But Freddy looked so sad."

"Alfredo," said Pops. "You'll come home as soon as possible. Don't worry. Everybody's just being careful."

"I know." What he really knew was that the Sox had a travel day today, so there was no game. But if he didn't get out by tomorrow night, he'd be stuck watching their road games in here. No good-luck popcorn in his lucky bowl, sitting in his lucky chair, wearing his '07 World Series hat with his favorite photo of "The Kid," aka Ted Williams, stuck inside. How could he start a rally without his KidLid? It was horrible timing to be stuck in this place, and besides that, he had no idea which nurse Mark had been talking about.

He bit into the sweet roll while keeping one eye on the door.

CHAPTER **14**

Pops was right about the tests. All afternoon, Stats was wheeled around the cardiac floor, where they not only took blood from his arm, but measured how fast the blood pumped into the little glass vial when they took it. He had breathing tests, stress tests, reflex tests, and heartbeat tests.

None of it was any fun.

Pops and Mark had stopped by for another visit, but Stats felt so tired, they left when he dozed off after dinner.

The next morning they were back.

"Test results look fine," said Pops, who did not quite sound as if he believed it. "A couple more today, Alfredo, then you should be coming home tomorrow."

"I was afraid of that."

"Doc says your heart is always running on low. That's why you can't exert yourself. He just wants to figure out the best thing to do for it."

Stats nodded. What could he say?

"See the sports page yet?" asked Mark.

"No."

"A guy at the *Boston Globe* thinks the Sox are falling into the same scenario they had back in 1919, when The Curse began. A few years of success, then *boom*, the big collapse."

"He said that? Where? Can you get me a copy?"

"Be right back." Mark hustled out.

Pops settled himself into a chair against the wall, then scooted it forward, but in so doing, he dropped a small pile of papers from his lap.

Stats could not see what the papers were, but the calculator among them caught his eye.

"Whatcha working on, Pops?"

"Oh, nothing. Just doing a little figuring."

"That's my department. What do you need to find out?"

"No, forget it. Not important." He tried to gather and sort the pages, placing a couple on the breakfast tray, then folded the rest up small enough to stuff into his shirt pocket.

Stats saw dollar signs. "Is that how much all this is gonna cost?" He knew about medical bills. Mark once mentioned that even though insurance paid most of Mama's bills, it still cost the family a ton.

"Oh, no, no." Pops shook his head. "Insurance is so much better nowadays. This is . . ."

Mark walked back in, distracting him a moment as he tossed the sports pages onto the bed.

Stats did not take them. "This is what, Pops?"

"Oh, like I say, it's nothing." Pops quickly folded the remaining pages into another square. "I just thought maybe our season tickets could help me pay down some of that debt."

Stats and Mark exchanged glances.

"How much are they worth?" asked Mark.

Pops seemed resigned to addressing the subject. He sat back. "Well, they're not cheap. They run about eleven thousand dollars a year."

"Oh, my gosh!" Stats cradled the sides of his head with his hands. "I never knew it was so high. That's five thousand five hundred dollars each!"

Pops shook his head. "No, no. Eleven thousand—that's per seat. It adds up to over twenty-two thousand potatoes a year."

"Whoa!"

"Well, they are very good seats."

"Does that include play-off and World Series tickets?" asked Mark.

"Oh, those. Don't ask."

Stats took a moment to imagine all the money Pops shelled out for the tickets. No wonder he couldn't afford to meet his bills.

Pops slumped. "Problem is, we need a lot more than those tickets are worth."

Stats thought a moment, knocking the numbers around his head. "Well, maybe not."

"Oh?" Pops smiled. "What do you suggest?"

"I know." Mark already had a plan. "Why don't you give the

tickets to the bill collector to sort of 'lose' your file? He's gotta be a Sox fan, right?"

Stats appreciated the ease of that solution. "Yeah, bribe the guy."

"Ah, geez," said Pops, "what am I raising, a couple of mobsters?"

"Well . . ." said Mark. "It could work."

Stats kept figuring. "No, but wait, Pops. I was thinking something else. What if you sold the tickets for what they're really worth?"

His father looked at him with a start. "They're worth more than what I pay?"

"Pops," said Mark. "These days? With the Sox selling out every game, every year since May 2003? If you sold those tickets on the open market, you could get, like, a thousand bucks a game. Maybe more. And there's eighty-one games a year, not counting the play-offs."

"That's a lot of money."

"Yeah," said Stats. "The seats all around us get resold all the time. And I've heard the buyers talk about the prices they paid. Never less than four hundred dollars per seat. And sometimes a lot more."

"Right," said Mark. "The Yankees series is worth a mint."

"Not only that," Stats began, even as his mind whirled in calculation, "if you sold the remaining tickets for this season and, say, the rights to next year's tickets—it could be enough to pay off the whole bill."

Pops brought his fingers to his chin. "That much, huh?" Then just as quickly, he waved his hand, shooshing the suggestion right out of his brain.

"I could never do that. It's not honest."

"Actually, Pops, it is," said Mark. "People do it all the time."

"People do a lot of things. But my own father never made a profit on those seats, and I'm not about to start looking at them like pieces of merchandise."

"But times are different now."

Pops was not having any of it. "No, no, forget I ever brought it up. Those seats are sacred. Either *we* use them, or I give them away. That's it. Besides, it's good for business. My vendors always give me their best deals. So the seats end up paying for themselves in the long run."

"But in the short run," Mark argued, "they could really help." Then he leaned over, picked up the newspaper, and gave it a flick. "Of course, if they keep losing like they are now, might be a time when you won't even get back what you paid for them."

CHAPTER 15

Stats spent two full days in the hospital and not only had to suffer watching Tuesday night's game against Baltimore on the small TV, but had to witness yet another loss.

On Wednesday night, home at last with his good-luck props, Stats watched the Sox barely preserve a lead, four runs whittled down to one by the ninth, to finally end their longest losing streak of the season at five games. They finished the night where they began, however. They now sat in third place, five games behind the Yankees, who had also won, and three behind the Rays.

In Baltimore on Thursday, Billee was scheduled to pitch. By then, Stats was feeling back to normal, and all he wanted to do was to cozy up to a bowl of Pops's popcorn, watch Billee stymie the Orioles, and enjoy the game.

In the bottom of the first, when Billee took the mound in Camden Yards, the Baltimore fans rose in support. It was heart-warming to see. Close-up shots even revealed hundreds of Red

Sox fans who were either from the area or die-hard supporters who had made the trip south from Boston, cheering and holding signs of encouragement.

BEAM ME UP BILLEE!

ORBITT'S IN A LEAGUE OF HIS ZONE.

And three girls bounced a long colorful sign saying, BILLEE'S NUTS! HERE COME DA LEAFLUTZ!

Well, the first batter for the Orioles should have taken note. He went down on strikes, thrashing wildly at "da leaflutz." Sadly, though, it was the last batter Billee would retire.

He got shelled. Nothing seemed to be working. They crushed his buckler, they hammered his dipster. Even when his leaflutz pitch induced a dribbler from the Orioles' cleanup hitter, the usually sure-handed Sandiego Gunsalvo at first base could not come up with it. And when he finally ran it down, he threw it away.

Run after run crossed the plate. Stats watched in horror. He saw poor Billee stand tall on the mound, looking up, repeatedly taking in deep breaths in order to calm himself and refocus. All to no avail.

Stats muted the sound.

Billee left the game in the first with only one out, bases loaded, and five runs across, four of them earned. The Orioles had batted around.

For once in his life, Stats was glad he was not at the ballpark. He did not watch the commercial that came on while the reliever warmed up, even though it was a Fen-Cent message featuring Matt Damon, Jimmy Fallon, and Drew Barrymore romanticizing about their days at Fenway. He did not watch any more of the game.

So much for feeling "normal." He could feel his heart straining under the stress of what he'd seen on TV, knowing what the Sox had just gone through.

"What's the deal with Billee, Freddy?" Mark asked as he walked into the room. "I just flipped on the radio, and he was already gone. Seems worse than just some curse. He say anything about feeling bad?"

"Not as far as I know."

"He got chewed, glued, and tattooed."

"I know. I saw. What am I supposed to do about it?"

"Hey, don't get mad at me."

"I'm not. But how should I know? I'm not his pitching coach. I'm just a kid he talks to every once in a while."

"Okay, sorry. I didn't mean to . . ."

"He was off balance, that's all. He's been like that. It happens. Doesn't mean he's a lousy pitcher."

"No one ever said that. Cheese, I feel bad, too, you know. I was just wondering."

Mark wandered out of the room.

Stats lay flat across the sofa cushions, the better to let the "sludge" pump through his slow-moving heart.

A lot of possibilities ran through his mind. None of them gave him any comfort. Billee could be sliding, could be swirl-draining his way into baseball oblivion. Countless pitchers had done the same. They come up out of nowhere, dominate for a year or two, then for some unexplainable reason, they lose whatever magic they had and slip out of sight with hardly anyone even noticing.

But if he were sick or hurt or overworked, that stuff was at least fixable. Even if it was the sophomore jinx everyone talks about, he could bounce back from that. But if this was truly the harbinger of a new Red Sox curse, and tonight Stats had no reason whatsoever to doubt it, the thing had to be broken right away. Or else it could go on for a *long* time.

CHAPTER 16

On Saturday morning, Stats and Mark took a break from Red Sox baseball, having suffered through yet another road loss on Friday. They clambered down the exterior stairway and, with the heavenly scent of fresh-cut grass filling their heads, they crossed Shawmut Avenue to the neighborhood ballfield where Mark's under-16 team, the Back Bay Bums, had a game.

It was a great day to be outside walking around, and with the Sox on the road, Stats and Mark would not need to rush off to Fenway as soon as the game ended.

Today Stats could, in fact, relax.

Arriving forty-five minutes before game time, Stats took his usual spot on the dugout bench, where he sat every game as the Bums' official team scorekeeper. Number 2 pencil ready, score-book spread open, he was all set to begin copying down the lineup Coach Carrigan had taped to the post.

And if Billee Orbitt was having a cursed year, Mark Pagano, who sat nearby sticking on black shade strips beneath his eyes, was having a stellar one.

In the prestigious Young Majors Baseball League, which had leagues set up in all twenty-eight Major League cities across the continent, Mark was held in the highest regard. He had patterned himself after the Breeze, and it had been an inspired choice. A true five-tool player, Mark had just lately mastered the bare-handed catch of the double play feed at second, which Ruíz used in order to gain a step.

"Guys, listen up," said Coach Carrigan, approaching the dugout. "One announcement before we start getting loose. We heard from YMBL headquarters in St. Louis last night. This year, because of the Fenway Park celebrations, there's going to be a national all-star team selected from YMBL players across the nation. They'll play against an all-star team from Japan for the YMBL World Championship."

"Whoa, they get to go to Japan?" said Jacky Kerwacki, a new kid from Lowell, who played either third base or was out in left field.

Coach frowned. "Hey, Kerwacki, I said listen. Not done yet. The American team will host the inaugural game. And the host field this year will be Fenway Park."

The team rumbled and hooted. "No way!" "Awesome." "I'm going."

"How do they pick the team?" asked Jonny Peskovich, the second baseman.

"They'll take the top player at each position plus two alternates and one designated hitter. Twelve guys in all."

Jimmy Zorro, a hard-hitting first baseman, asked, "How do they decide who's the top player at every position?"

"Stats."

Stats looked up. "Yeah, Coach?"

"No, I mean your stats will determine your ranking. Just like in the Major Leagues with the Golden Glove and the Silver Slugger awards. Only difference is, your offensive and defensive stats will be combined into one final ranking. And, look. We still have nine games to go, so a lot can happen."

There was a low group hum of comprehension as the players processed the coach's news.

"What if you play more than one position?" asked Kerwacki.

"As far as I can tell, they'll take your fielding numbers at each spot and combine them to get your final stats. Whichever position you played the most innings at is your main spot, and that's the category you'll compete in. And by tomorrow night, each league will have the stats of their top five guys at each spot posted on the national website. That list gets updated daily from then on." He clapped his hands. "Okay, 'at's it. Let's warm up."

The players jumped off the bench and scrambled to the outfield grass. All except for Mark. He waited until they'd all left, then spoke softly to Stats. "Wonder where I am on the shortstop list."

"You're number one for sure."

"No, I don't mean for our league. I mean across the country."

"I'll find out as soon as the other numbers are posted."

Mark nodded. "Not that I care. Gotta be a long shot."

"Are you kidding? You're right in there for sure. And Fenway Park! Representing America's best? Come on!"

"Yeah, whatever. Could be a hundred guys in front of me."

Stats knew the game Mark was playing now. Act as if you don't care. Don't get your hopes up—at least, don't ever let anyone else know how high your hopes really are.

"Well, have a good game," he said. "Now you're really playing for something big."

Mark rose, grabbed his glove. "We'll see. Like Coach said. It's all gonna come down to one thing." He flicked his brother's hat brim. "Stats."

The game that day was raucous. Playing before a great neighborhood crowd, both teams hit well, though neither side had pitched well. Finally, the Back Bay Bums came out on top of a 12–11 slugfest.

One thing Stats loved about these games was being among the fans who came to watch. These people were baseball enthusiasts, sportsmen, students of the game. It was not just family members, but shopkeepers, mailmen, next-door neighbors, and teachers of the players who attended. That meant both teams heard cheers from both sides for a particularly difficult defensive play or a heads-up baserunning maneuver. For instance, in the third inning when Mark rounded first and spied a flat-footed left fielder double-pumping the relay, he took an extra base, which prompted knowing shouts and compliments from all around.

Such plays not only earned respect and general enthusiasm, but brought the happy fans back game after game.

And why not? Boston was a fantastic baseball town, and overall, the fans were among the most—if not *the* most—knowledgeable in the land. Stats only wished he would witness some of this local sportsmanship when things got rough for Billee and the Sox at Fenway.

CHAPTER 17

Meanwhile, the curse got worse.

The Red Sox finished the weekend series in Toronto dropping two out of three against the Blue Jays. On Monday night, the Sox used four pitchers during a game in Tampa that Stats wished he had recorded so he could have simply deleted it without bothering to watch. Fireballer Cedro Marichal started. He was wild in the strike zone, got bombed, and left in the third inning with two outs, two on, and five runs across. From there, it only went downhill.

On Tuesday night, Billee was scheduled to pitch, but the Sox decided to go with their hottest pitcher, Will "Cannonball" Jackman, instead. Fortunately, even on four days' rest, Cannonball pitched well enough to win, lasting six and giving up only four runs, three earned, to stop the Red Sox's slide. Even so, the Sox now sat six games out of first.

Since Stats had donned his lucky KidLid halfway through tonight's game, he wore it to bed, too, hoping it might help sustain the team's luck.

It didn't. The Sox lost two more in Tampa before finally returning home for a game on Friday, when they would face the Kansas City Royals. Billee was now scheduled to start against the Royals on Saturday.

During all the hubbub, as Pops called it, Stats had also managed to see Doc Roberts, and, once again, things could have gone better. While the doc checked out Stats's heart, a look of concern clouded his face.

"What is it?" said Pops.

Doc hesitated a moment before he answered. "Angelo, I want you and Freddy to stop by Children's Hospital next week and have them rerun a few tests." He rose. "Nothing to worry about. But I just want to be sure. Then I want to see you two back here once I get a look at the results."

Nothing to worry about, thought Stats, and he was eager to leave it at that.

Pops, however, carried the doctor's cloud of concern all the way home.

On that Friday afternoon, while Stats tended the kettles at Papa Pagano's, he monitored the street for Billee. He was bursting to tell him everything he'd learned about quartz and amethyst crystals and bogs, even though he was not quite certain what any of it meant.

Meanwhile, the game day patrons vented their frustrations over the Red Sox's road trip, which had left them seven games out of first. It had been quite a fall after being at the top of their division only two weeks before.

"Total meltdown, that's what it is," said Announcer Bouncer in his bellowing voice. "Reminds me of 1986. And I don't mean the Game Six fiasco. I mean Chernobyl."

"Ah, it's still early in the season," said Mark, not wanting Bouncer's comments to contaminate the line. "Over the last hundred years, we've pretty much seen it all."

"But over the last ten years," said Lulu, another regular customer, "this stretch is right up there with the worst."

"Should've picked up some better talent during the winter," Bouncer added. "We get charged an arm and a leg for tickets to these games. The least they could've done was to go out and buy us a few arms and a couple of legs, right, guys?"

Everyone laughed at that, but there didn't seem to be any relief in it. Stats knew as well as anyone that witnessing your home team fall, one painful game at a time, from first to fourth in their division, behind New York, Tampa, and Toronto, is not an easy thing to laugh off.

But he simply kept busy, wrapping up and passing along the last of Bouncer's ten-dog order without uttering a word.

Besides, what could he say? That the team was truly cursed? Who would want to hear that?

So for now, Stats focused on checking up and down Yawkey for Billee's arrival.

Sadly, the only other person on planet earth who shared the depth of Stats's concern over the Sox did not make his way to the stand that day. Ah, he's busy, thought Stats. Other things to worry about. After all, he's pitching tomorrow.

For some reason, though, during the game, Stats could not shake his nervousness. He rocked in his seat with his scorebook on his lap for the first two hours, anxiously watching while Will "Cannonball" Jackman, with his hard-sinking forkball, held the Royals to three runs through seven. It turned out to be a seesaw nail-biter that the Sox ultimately won 6–5. As luck would have it, though, the Yankees had won as well, so the Sox did not gain any ground.

After the game, Stats headed straight to the bull pen area and sat in the seats above, waiting for the park to clear, just on the off chance he could spy Billee heading for his meditational haunt.

When Mark finally appeared at his side, he bugged Stats to go home.

Knowing that it could be a long wait for Billee to show up— if he *does at all*—Stats reluctantly agreed to join his brother and troop on home.

Besides, tomorrow was another day, with two great games on tap. First off, Mark would go into his morning match versus Cambridge ranked third nationwide in the YMBL shortstop category. A really strong game might actually put him on top.

Then that night, Billee would take the hill against the Royals, a team he always did well against.

Maybe things weren't so bad after all. Hey, as Mark had said, still a lot of baseball left to go. Who says it can't get better?

CHAPTER 18

Saturday morning, at the Cambridge Cavemen baseball park, Stats mentioned Mark's status to Coach Carrigan, who took the good news in stride.

"I just hope Mark doesn't start pressing," said the coach, pacing in the visitors' dugout as the Bums warmed up. "I want to see him get back to driving the ball up the middle. Last game, he was out in front, yanking it."

Stats hummed a quiet response. He knew Mark was pressing. How could he not? They'd even talked about it. The thing was, as Mark explained, "Telling yourself to be patient at the plate and being patient are two different bananas."

Mark's first at bat Saturday against the Cambridge ace, Frannie Matthews, proved the point. For the first time in seven games, he struck out. And for a pure contact hitter like Mark, striking out was not a good sign.

"I got anxious," he said. "Chased one outside. I wish they would just pitch to me. What are they afraid of?"

Well, now, thought Stats. Twelve home runs, forty-seven runs batted in, a .514 batting average—just to name a few.

"Get 'em next time," mumbled Stats, regretting he had to pencil in a K next to his brother's name.

Later on, he penciled another K, this one in reverse, to indicate Mark had been caught looking at the third strike. But between those strikeouts, Mark scratched out two singles, going two-for-four on the day, and wound up scoring the winning run. Yes, he was nervous, pressing. But he was still Mark.

That afternoon, Stats did not bother watching for Billee to appear at Papa Pagano's, since he was due to pitch, and the last time he had stopped by on a game day—well, let's just say it did not improve his luck much. So Stats was not disappointed when his expectations proved to be the case.

He spent the last few minutes before game time running the recyclables to their respective bins and humming a song about how good times never seemed so good.

What Stats could not have expected was to hear from Bull Brickner, the usher, that the Red Sox had just scratched Billee from the lineup.

"Clubhouse says it's a groin muscle," said Bull. "Paolo thinks it happened during warm-ups."

"A pulled muscle?" said Stats. "Doesn't sound like Billee. He stretches for hours."

Bull shrugged. "I think they're gonna take Woods out of the bull pen and have him start, or else maybe move Beer Can Byrd up a day."

Stats hustled back to share the news with Mark and Pops. But by then, they, too, had heard the announcement on TV.

"Did they say if he's on the DL?" asked Stats.

Mark shook his head. "No, they said it'd be day-to-day."

"So who's pitching?"

Pops seemed to know. "They're moving Byrd up in the rotation."

"Yeah," said Mark. "I think they're hoping to get five out of Beer Can, then go to the pen."

Stats shook his head. "So Byrd's pitching on three days' rest. This can't be good."

"One of those things," said Pops. "Why don't you two go on in. Catch the national anthem. I heard they got Chick Corea playing a jazzy electric piano with a local kid, Maria Tecce, singing. Supposed to be sultry." He waved his hand. "Go on. Tell me about it."

If sultry meant old-fashioned, then it was, and Stats sort of liked it. But he missed seeing Billee take center stage.

"Maybe you can find out what happened after the game," said Mark.

"Hope so."

That was not to be. Billee had spent the evening in the clubhouse getting extra attention for his muscle strain.

And when the Sox left town on Thursday, after a short six-game home stand, without Stats ever getting a chance to connect with Billee, his heart reminded him daily that things were not "balancing out" very well. Sure, Pops had handed out the tickets to several business associates for the last few games. That happened from time to time. Sure, Billee had rehabilitation work to focus on, so he was in the clubhouse a lot. And by the time the home stand ended, with three wins and three losses, they had simply not been in the same place at the same time.

But every time Stats asked himself whether he should be concerned about the new curse growing a little stronger each day, his heart would slow down, engorge a bit, then double pump. Pure stress.

To Stats, it was a sure sign that something bad was brewing.

As June's first week of baseball rolled along, Stats tried to stay as positive as possible and look for any signs that things might be balancing out for both Billee and the Red Sox.

Sadly, none appeared.

Boston's current ace, Cannonball Jackman, the only starter with a winning record, had been placed on the DL with a sore shoulder on June 5. So to start that Tuesday's game, the Sox promoted left-hander Howie Woods from the bull pen. As a reliever, Woods had been known to throw the kind of smoke that finished off most hitters. In his new starting role, however, he could not finish the fourth inning.

Since they were playing in Oakland, Stats followed the game

online as well as on TV. By the third inning, the fans in the blogosphere had again turned ugly. The virtual boos they had first aimed at Woods morphed into barely censored catcalls, taunts, and sneers for the entire team. That continued until the bitter end, with the Sox dropping a lopsided wartsfest, 9–1.

By the end of the weekend series in Seattle, Billee had yet to see any action at all, and Stats had seen enough. He'd seen so many "lost-in-the-lights" doubles, booted double-play balls, and run-scoring *un*holy rollers to become obsessed with this new curse. He talked about it constantly with Mark and wanted nothing more than to find a way to undo the thing, no matter what it took—*now*.

CHAPTER 19

The following Tuesday, June 12, the "Dead Sox," as the bloggers had already begun to call them, were once again back at Fenway hosting Tampa. Having just been swept in Oakland and Seattle, tonight they were hoping to halt a seven-game losing streak.

During that time, the Red Sox pitching rotation had undergone a slew of changes. Stats wasn't certain, but according to a few websites, Billee was healthy enough to start and was, in fact, due to pitch on Wednesday.

It was all rumors, though, since the Spacebird didn't show up at the Red Hots stand on Tuesday to visit or report or confirm anything. Was Billee just going to let the curse run its course? Had he gone on to other ideas without mentioning them? Or was he so immersed in his struggles on the mound and the team's overall downspin that the strain of it completely absorbed him? If any of these were the case, Stats would not blame him one bit. But *where* was he?

Then, on Wednesday afternoon, something strange happened.

Just as Stats had finished helping to set up the stand at the ballpark, Paolo Williams, the groundskeeper, came outside and said Red Gruffin wanted to see him.

"What for?" asked Stats.

"Beats me, Freddy Ballgame. Said he had something for you."

Well, as long as it's not a cigar stub to chew on, thought Stats.

He found Ol' Red sitting all alone inside the nearly deserted upper-deck seats above the infield on the first-base side. And though Red watched closely from the moment Stats emerged from the tunnel, he said nothing until Stats greeted him from the aisle two feet away.

"Hi, Mr. Gruffin. Paolo said—"

"Hey!" Ol' Red cut him off and aimed his cigar butt at Stats's nose. "You didn't hear this from me. Got it?"

Stats did not even offer a nod, afraid to acknowledge he'd heard that much.

Ol' Red peered around the park, then shifted forward in his seat.

"Back in April 2008, just before opening day, a little girl and her school class was here on a tour of the park, okay? She walked right along the rail there." He pointed past the bottom row. "The situation was, a mama hawk had a nest right up there in them rafters." He indicated the ceiling of the upper deck. "Had two eggs she'd been brooding. Now, the kid was doing nothing but minding her own beeswax, and that mama bird come swooping down, claws out, and strafed that poor girl's head like a jet pilot running touch-and-goes."

He sat back. "Well, she wasn't hurt bad. Scratched up some. Scared, mostly. Which was the point. Mama bird just wanted to send a message. But the next thing you know, animal rescue was out here taking down the nest, eggs and all. Now, I don't agree with that. Them hawks do us a service keeping down the rodent population. Besides, I happened to see 'em living in that nest. Right after we won the '07 World Series. Good-luck sign, far as I'm concerned. But everybody's worried about lawsuits, ain't they? Anyways, after that I had to crack the whip. Every year, baby birds or not, we cleared out the nests. I *never* felt good about it. But . . ." He shrugged and left it at that.

"Anyways, you seemed interested in rats. And like I told you, if I thought of something . . ." He cocked his head and narrowed an eye. He held the look until Stats had to blink. "All right?"

Ol' Red pushed himself up, thrust a black leather work boot into the aisle, stepped out, and kept on going. Had Stats not jumped back, Ol' Red would've run him over.

Stats watched the crotchety old man clop down the steps and onto the landing. Crotchety with a heart of gold.

"All right," said Stats, weighing the news. "All right."

CHAPTER **20**

At game time, Stats paused with Mark at the top of the aisle while the Mighty Mighty Bosstones played the national anthem. Afterward, as Stats settled into his field-level seat for the game, he was so happy to finally see Billee Orbitt scratching up the mound and going through his pregame rituals. Even if most fans had tired of the show—that is, they had tired of Billee's focus ritual not being connected to, say, ten straight wins for a pennant contender, as he had done during one stretch in 2011— Stats still loved to watch Billee Orbitt slip into his O-Zone, as some fans still called it.

During the game, however, he slipped even further—into the "Oh, no!" zone. As painful as it was to watch, Stats did find comfort in at least something. Billee had done his best. He had worked as hard as Stats had ever seen him work. He hit his targets, he changed speeds, he worked the corners, he held runners close, even picking off a guy on first.

But he only lasted three and two-thirds innings. And three

of those were struggles. Why? Pure, unadulterated *bad-luck runs*. The two errors to begin the fourth were only the final examples. The ground rule double that came next, of course, was on Billee, whose ERA, despite a ton of unearned BLRs, had ballooned from 3.13 to 9.50 in the past four weeks.

What hurt Stats the most, however, was the booing. The loud, boisterous, angry boos that greeted Billee from the second inning on cut into Stats as deeply as they seemed to affect the performance of his friend on the mound.

Each time Billee tromped around or held the ball in front of his face and talked to himself, the hecklers would go nuts.

"Throw the ball, Birdbrain!"

"Pretend like you've played this game before!"

Even his world-famous leaflutz pitch brought ridicule. "Where'd you learn to throw that, Space Case? On the moon?"

In four weeks' time, the Red Sox had gone from being tied with the Yankees to being eleven games off the pace and nine games behind Tampa.

Even so, thought Stats, why do people get like that? Now is the time the Sox needed them most. Besides, it's only the middle of June. Lots of baseball to go.

After the game, Mark urged Stats to make a quick exit. "Billee won't be leaving the clubhouse tonight, Freddy."

Stats had already checked twice. He pulled in a deep breath. "I know. But let me go down and take one more look, okay?"

Stats finally caught a glimpse of Billee's bare feet protruding from the bull pen.

"Just give me a minute," he shouted to Mark.

He ran to the front row and called down to the pen.

Billee poked his head out. "Come over this way," he said. "I'm not coming out. I'll bring you over the lip."

Stats slid underneath the railing just above the pen, and Billee reached up to swing him all the way in.

"Dude," said Billee as Stats hit the ground. "We've been booed so bad, I'm afraid to show my face around here. I hope you scored *some*thing. I need any shred of hope you can give me. The cosmic momentum of this deal is galactic. I tell you, it's taking us all down."

"I think I might have something. Not sure, but back in 2008, just before opening day, this mother hawk swooped down from her nest and attacked a girl here on a field trip. Scratched her head up and everything."

"Well, that hawk was just protecting her young."

"Yeah, sure, but Ol' Red says they had to call animal rescue to come and take the nest away. And ever since then, they take down every hawk nest they find."

"They do? So that's what we're dealing with."

"What?"

"A hawk's nest monster." Billee winked and slapped the visor on Stats's hat.

"Billee, focus!"

"Okay, okay."

"Because the point is, ever since then, the Sox have never come close to another World Series."

Stats let Billee digest the info while he tapped his eXfyle. Up came a historical site for Fenway Park. "And, okay, one last thing." He showed the screen to Billee.

"This article is a hundred years old, from back in 1912, the year they built the ballpark. The mayor was a guy named Honey Fitz, and he gave a little speech at the dedication ceremony."

Stats read part of it out loud.

"This base ball playing field represents the sort of exceptional community involvement I support with all my heart. From the days of swamps and marshland where the only local occupants might have been a few frogs, muskrats, hoot owls, and hawks, to the more recent days of industry and all its dust and grime, this plot of land has come a long way. Today, with the completion of his improvements upon this site, Mr. John Taylor has given the city of Boston a sporting facility of national merit. May it shine forever."

Stats looked up. Billee sat grim-faced with his arms pressed against his chest.

"It seems like all this fits together, right?" said Stats. "I mean, there must be a connection . . . somehow."

Billee nodded. "There is."

He rose. He said nothing as he walked to the bull pen fence and rested his arms on top, facing home. For a while he simply looked out over the ballfield.

"Can you see it?"

"See what?" said Stats.

Billee pointed across the diamond. "From ancient times, the balance of nature on this land meant a natural park, right here. White oaks and silver maples towering out of the marshlands, like we had out where I grew up."

"Like you saw in that dream you told me about."

"When did I tell you about that dream?"

"You know. In the hospital."

"*When* was that?"

"Oh, never mind. I think I was dreaming."

Billee stared. "You dreamed my dream?"

"Were you flying over Fenway?"

Billee nodded.

Stats opened his mouth wide. "Whoa."

Billee stood stunned. "Oh, my goggles. Dude, I don't believe that happened! Okay, okay. This is big. This tells me something. On this land, on this sacred ground we're standing on, there has always been a balance. There's been a special energy, a . . ."

". . . a *chi*?"

Billee grinned. "Exactamundo. And what I mean is, it connects me and you as much as anything else." He knelt down, facing Stats, taking him by the shoulders. "Stat Man, this is our big break. No wonder the first curse lasted eighty-six years. It's not the ballpark that's out of whack. It's not even the team. It's the balance of nature. It's the chi. The hawks! That's our wing flap."

He turned toward the right-field bleachers and shouted, "We need to bring back the hawks!"

CHAPTER 21

As with any diagnosis, naming the problem and solving the problem were, of course, two different things. Billee was convinced that the natural chi must be returned to Fenway by way of bringing back the displaced hawks. Fine, thought Stats, but how?

Then an idea hit. As he and Mark rode the Route 8 bus home that night, he announced, "When I see Billee tomorrow, I'm going to suggest that we get boxes of rats and frogs and dump them all around Fenway Park. What do you think?"

"What, you think that's gonna attract some hawks?" said Mark. "Balance things out?"

Stats shrugged. "I guess. Gotta think of something."

"If the hawks were so important to the winning energy at Fenway, why haven't we heard about them before? Wouldn't you think that they would've noticed big imbalances at least a few times in the past? I've read all about 1967 and '78 and '86—all those heartbreak years—but nobody ever said, 'Hey, guys, look at all these rats running around. Better get some hawks over here, pronto.'"

"Yeah, well, maybe that's because they used poisons instead, the way they always did. But Red Gruffin did complain about the rats in '86. It's just that nobody ever thought of using the natural approach."

The bus jerked to a stop. Mark rose and grabbed his bag. "You mean, until 2004?"

"Well, even that wasn't on purpose, but, yeah, that's what me and Red think. That year, with all the construction, the hawks were left alone to do their job." Stats pushed himself up. "And in 2007, Ol' Red actually saw a nest."

As they headed to the exit, Mark thanked John Dog, the Route 8 driver, as he always did.

"Yeah," Stats added, "thanks, Mr. Daemon. See ya next time."

The driver casually tucked a hank of long loose hair behind his ear. "You cowboys take care."

Stats followed his brother off the bus. They walked quietly for a while, approaching their block.

"Well, in a, you know, ecological kind of way," said Mark, "it sorta makes sense, what you guys are thinking. But on the other hand, Freddy, remember, Billee is pretty well known for being about six outs shy of a complete game. So, you know . . ."

"Don't worry. I know it sounds loopy. But at least it feels like I'm doing something. I mean, what if it turns out we could've done something to help the Sox, and we didn't?"

"I hear you. I'm just saying, don't go too overboard on all this, okay? They don't call him Spacebird for nothing."

Stats let that comment stew as they arrived home. Silently, they climbed the stairs. Creaking open the front door, Stats saw that Pops was still up. He had several manila folders and sheets of paper spread out all over their big mahogany table.

He did not greet them with his usual exuberance.

"How did it go, boys?"

That question alone was surprising. Didn't he know?

"They lost," said Stats.

"Ah, geez." In what appeared to be a bit of guarded stealth, Pops cleared the table with quick hands, not bothering to sort, and slid the papers together, placing them inside a single folder. Then he set all the folders on a shelf in the alcove facedown. Turning back, his mood seemed to have brightened.

"Had a little success with my chili dog buns today. Added some rye flour, and they held together a lot better. Think I'm getting closer."

Mark joined Pops in his elevated mood. "Hey, that's good to hear. No more soggy middles." Playfully, he slapped his father on his rather abundant middle and pulled back, in a boxing pose.

Pops only grinned while tapping his knuckles against his head. "Knock on wood."

"Let us try it out next," said Stats.

"You bet," said Pops. "I'll have a new batch ready tomorrow. Oh, and Alfredo, don't forget. We have that doctor's appointment in the morning."

"Yeah, I know," he said, although he had, until then, forgotten.

They each exchanged tired good nights and headed to their rooms. On the way, Stats sneaked a glance at the upside-down folders on the shelf, though they remained a mystery. Was Pops working on another plan to raise money? he wondered. What would he think of selling this time?

True to his word, Pops had both chili dog buns and hotcakes ready for Stats and Mark as they stumbled out of their room the next morning.

"And, hey," said Pops, once the boys found their way to the table, "there was something I forgot to mention. After you two left to go inside the park last night, a couple of the Boston Red Sox people stopped by. They said they wanted me to record one of those centennial messages for the Fenway Fever celebration."

"Whoa, Pops!" Mark drummed the table. "That is huge. What are you gonna say?"

"I said I'd think about it and let them know."

"No, no," said Mark, "I mean on the JumboTron. You definitely have to tell the Sox you'll do it. You just have to figure out your message. We can help."

"Yeah," said Stats, "it'll be fun."

"Well, see, that's what I want to talk to you boys about." Pops made his way around the table, a griddle full of Wenham Lake blueberry pancakes in one hand and a spatula in the other.

"Those Fen-Cent messages, I've seen a bunch of them. They play 'em on TV during the games, and I'm always thinking, the problem is, it's all grown-ups. I keep wishing they'd get some kids up there for some of those announcements instead of all these old people talking about the old days all the time. To you boys, someday these will be the old days, eh?"

He dumped a leaning tower of hotcakes onto Mark's plate.

"So what I decided was, I'm passing the honor on to you two. What do you say?"

Mark hunched forward, head bent. He held the hot maple syrup tin by its wooden handle, but did not pour. "You sure you wanna do that? I don't exactly have any stories to tell." He looked up. "You're the guy who runs the best hot dog stand in Boston. Zillions of people know you. Come on, Pops. You do it."

Pops turned to Stats. "What say you, Alfredo?"

Stats cut down into his buttered stack with a fork edge. "I'll do it."

"You will?" Mark stared wide-eyed.

Stats shrugged. "I love Fenway, I love the Red Sox, I love baseball. I could come up with something, I guess."

Pops cast a reading glance. "It's up to you, Alfredo. No one is saying you have to."

"I know. But it'll be sort of like a webcam, right? You just stare at the camera and talk. I've done stuff like that before."

"So should I call Mr. Lucchesi and tell him?"

"Yeah," said Stats, stabbing his cuttings and raising his fork. "Go ahead, let him know."

The worst I could do, he figured, is fall flat on my face. But, hey, the way the Sox are playing, who's gonna notice?

CHAPTER 22

Stats and Pops arrived at Doc Roberts's office ten minutes late for an appointment neither was in a hurry to attend. Today there would be no tests. Today they would receive no new results. The facts were in. This meeting centered on prognosis—that is, what to do next.

"As I have said before," Doc began, "vagus nerve disorders can be tricky."

Strewn across the cluttered desk in front of him, Stats could see medical charts and printed material, as if Doc had done some recent research on the matter.

"In children," he continued, "we generally let things go forward awhile because in many cases they can improve on their own."

Strike one, thought Stats. His "defects" were still in their near-original condition, as far as he could tell.

Doc focused on Pops. "In this case, Angelo, we see that

Alfredo's condition is actually slipping somewhat. That is to say, the episodes of heartbeat irregularity seem to be increasing."

Strike two, thought Stats.

"So what can we do?" Pops shifted in the small chair and leaned forward, pressing his palms into his knees.

"One fairly common approach is to implant a pacemaker. A simple regulator will catch the arrhythmia right away and signal the heart so it returns to a normal beat rate."

"A pacemaker?" said Pops. "That's for old guys, isn't it? They use those on kids?"

"In some cases we do, and the results can be exactly what we want."

"But they might not be . . ."

"In children there are some risks that most older patients don't face."

Strike three. Stats already felt defeated.

Finally, Doc Roberts looked at him. "Alfredo is in the bottom five percentile for kids his age in weight, and he's in the bottom ten percentile for boys his age in height."

Stats knew these stats by heart, so to speak. The old height-weight data. Yes, he was a flea, the tiniest kid in his class. So what? That condition by itself did not affect his happiness. What affected his happiness was when people pointed it out.

Pops cast a sideward glance. "He's slight, I know."

Slight was a nice word, thought Stats. Pops always knew how to go easy on a guy.

"Right," said the doctor. "And that's not uncommon for a

boy with bradyarrhythmia. That is, a slow heart rate. But once a strong steady rate is established, it would go a long way toward allowing Alfredo here to attain a more normal stature and enjoy a more active lifestyle."

Would it allow me to play baseball? Stats wondered. He did not dare ask, however. Even though Doc would probably say yes, there was no way he would be imagining the kind of baseball Stats had in mind.

"Risks, though," said Pops. "You said there might be risks."

"A while back the Boston Children's Hospital and the Department of Pediatrics at Harvard Medical concluded a twenty-year study looking into long-term outcomes for children with pacemaker implants. They found that younger patients, specifically those under the age of twelve, had significantly higher incidents of complications."

Technically, I'm over the age of twelve, thought Stats, who was born on Valentine's Day in the year 2000.

He quickly calculated his exact age at 12.3333 years, his last birthday having been precisely four months ago.

"And the number one factor," Doc continued, "contributing to problems is the physical size of the patient."

Stats slumped and folded his arms.

"Another contributing factor is future growth that may cramp or dislodge the unit. Overall, physical activity tends to increase, which is good, but with that comes the risk of displacing the unit's electrical wiring where it connects to the heart."

Pops sat back. Stats studied the floor, deciphering what he had just heard. A pacemaker connects straight to the heart? Well, he guessed it would have to, in order to send the electronic impulses that sparked the heart when the vagus nerve didn't. But was it always coming loose? Would he have to have operation after operation for the next ten years? If so, then wouldn't it be best if he just waited until he was older?

"So what are you saying, Doc?" Pops, too, needed clarity.

"There's no clear-cut course of action here, Angelo. Every patient is unique, with a host of considerations."

"But . . ."

"But, all in all, I'd like you both to consider going ahead with the implant. In the long run, I think it would be best."

"What about all the risks?"

Doc nodded. "Even taking them into consideration, I see a pacing device as the better choice."

"Better than . . . ?"

"Better than doing nothing." Once again he turned to Stats. "Freddy, up until now, we've always taken a wait and see approach. But as it is, things are not improving."

Stats knew that as well as anyone. This year had been the roughest yet, no matter how much he had tried to downplay it.

He just needed to be clear on one thing. "If we go ahead with the pacemaker," he asked, "what's the number one risk?"

"That it fails when you really need it."

Stats nodded. "And if we just let things go along the way they are?"

"To be honest, Freddy, the biggest risk is still the same. Your heart fails when you really need it. Of course, that happens to everyone on earth eventually. The only thing is, without the operation, that failure would most likely come sooner than later."

CHAPTER 23

Wrapping up a quick series with the Rays—with three devastating losses—the Sox again hit the road, this time to Minnesota, where they won two in a row against the Twins to finally snap their losing streak at *ten games*.

"Too bad it had to happen in Minnesota," said Mark as he joined Stats at the kitchen table to finish off a carton of rocky road ice cream before going to bed. "Sox fans need to see a few good ones like that right here, close-up."

Stats agreed, but knew it was better than nothing. "Maybe playing away from all that booing helped. Especially if they can string a few more wins together and get things figured out."

"Unless they're just plain cursed," said Mark. "Then no matter how good they look, even if they climb back on top, they'll never win the Big One."

"Don't have to remind me. But to be totally honest, I'd settle for a heartbreak season, even another 2011, over no chance at all."

Passing through the parlor, Stats noticed Pops was once again busy with a file of papers.

"What're you working on?"

This time, Pops made no effort to hide his project.

"I ran into Anton Martinelli the other day. Turns out, his brother-in-law is a big-time business lawyer. So I told him about this mess I'm in."

"We're in," corrected Mark, who had fallen in behind Stats.

"Yeah, everybody, I suppose. Any rate, he phones up his brother-in-law right there in the street and gives him the quick lowdown. The guy tells him I have two options."

"You're not going to sell the seats, are you?"

"Wouldn't help if I did. He says in my situation, I can either walk away from everything and declare bankruptcy or I can sell off my business interests and hope to get enough to pay off my debts."

It took Stats a moment for the news to register. The "business interests" would be Papa Pagano's Red Sox Red Hots, which had been in the family even longer than the season tickets.

"What does he mean, declare bankruptcy?" asked Mark.

"It means we go belly-up. Lose everything we have except the house."

"What if we just take out a loan or something and pay the bills off over time?"

"Markangelo, I'm borrowed up to my eyeballs as it is. Look, I got the whole lowdown. If I don't pay these guys off, the business goes to auction. And an auction won't bring anywhere near as much as I could get if I sold out now under my own terms, without the pressure."

"Now? As in . . . ?"

"As in this week. ASAP. I don't have a choice. We got things coming up."

"Things coming up" was Pops's way of saying that he and Stats had decided to take the doctor's advice. Stats was scheduled to go into surgery on Tuesday, June 26, less than two weeks away. And insurance would not cover everything. As Pops had learned with Mama's illness, he would need any extra money that the sale of Papa Pagano's would provide in order to help with the additional expenses.

"How much is the business worth?" It seemed so strange to hear Mark voice that question—the idea felt so absurd. But now that it had been proffered, Stats wanted to know, too.

"That's what I'm working on tonight. Getting all my income and expenses sorted out. The guy I talked to said if my receipts are what I say they are, he could get me something like a hundred fifty thousand dollars. Two hundred, tops."

"Whoa," said Stats. "That's a lot of money."

Pops let out a sigh. "Seems like it. But afterwards, we end up with no income at all and only a little bit of cash."

"Wait a minute," said Mark. "Which guy told you this? The lawyer?"

"No, no, I saw a business broker on Friday. Another buddy of Anton's. But, listen, the guy is sharp. So was the lawyer. I know I could go all around town and get everybody's opinion, and this and that, but they'd all say pretty much the same thing. Sell now, at your price. Pay off that mountain of debt. Start over. Breathe easy."

"Start over doing what?"

"Who knows? Open up the grocery store." He shrugged. "I mean, we keep the house, if we can still make the payments. And that's part of the house."

Whether Pops was serious about that idea or not, the mere mention of the store took most of the fire out of Mark. "We'll make the house payments," he said. "Even if I have to go out and get another job."

"Me too," said Stats.

Pops shook his head. "No, no, no. Look, we're getting ahead of ourselves here. Let's just take it step by step, and we'll figure everything out."

Stats let it go. So did Mark. Pops had made a reasoned decision. Stats hated the idea of selling Papa Pagano's. But Pops probably did, too. At any rate he had weighed all the options.

Maybe it was just like the lawyer had suggested. It's time for Pops to breathe easy.

CHAPTER 24

Sunday, June 17, was Father's Day, and as they had done for the past three years, Mark and Stats took Pops out to lunch at Angie's Ristoránte for her specialty, spaghetti and pork chops.

On the way there, they passed a neighborhood regular, Frazzled Harry, who tended to haunt the alcoves of vacant storefronts while subtly "asking" for money.

"Good day, Mr. Pagano. Say there, boys."

"Frazzey Harry," said Pops with a lilt in his voice, "you're out bright and early this fine day. Any sure bets coming up at Suffolk Downs this season that a fellow might 'invest in'?"

Harry squinted into the sunlight. "No, no. None yet."

Years ago, Frazzled Harry trained thoroughbreds at the famed racetrack in East Boston and had produced several winners. Then he hit a rough patch "down the stretch," as Pops called it.

"But I'll keep my ear to the ground," said Frazzled Harry. "Meantime, I'm just happy to greet my lady friends heading to mass at St. Francis. You know, they never forget a friend."

What everyone knew was that Harry could always glad-hand a few dollars smiling at the church crowd on Sundays, which was the only day Stats ever saw him.

"Well, good luck to you," said Pops, who extended his hand. Harry did the same. They shook.

Stats could not figure out when Pops had managed to palm a folded twenty-dollar bill, but somehow in the last few steps, he had done exactly that. Upon hearing paper rustle, Stats caught a quick glimpse as Pops slipped Harry the money during the handshake.

Nothing new there. Pops rarely missed a chance to help a guy out who had hit a rough patch. In fact, he had always told his sons to "take care of your family—that's why God gave them to you." The only problem Stats could see with Pops's philosophy was the size of his family. Even now, when he knew he was deep in debt, anyone he met was automatically in it.

At the restaurant, Angie was all smiles, as if she'd been waiting for them to appear. Of course, she had been, since Mark had stopped in the day before to set things up.

"Happy Father's Day," she said while hugging her black vinyl menus against a silky red top. "Your favorite table is all set." She led them to the front window.

"Angelina," said Pops, "every table in here is my favorite."

She beamed, then passed out the menus as everyone took a seat. "Tell me now, Mr. Pagano, how is it coming with the dog pockets? I am ready for a new batch to bake."

The hot dog pockets Pops had been trying to perfect were often test-baked in Angie's commercial oven, to give him an idea of their quality in a large run.

"I'm hoping to get you another batch this week," said Pops. "This time I'm adding rye flour. I read it helps the ingredients bond together better. Hold their shape more." He rolled his fists around each other.

"Umm, this process sounds to be so scientific," she said, nodding, matching Pops in her earnestness.

She stepped back. "I bring the water." She left.

"Pops," said Mark. "I think Angie's got a crush on you."

"Yeah," Stats teased, "you're *so* scientific."

"Hush, hush, now, with all that." He looked toward the kitchen to judge Angie's distance. Satisfied, he turned back. "She comes to this country, opens her own place, just like your grandfather, eh? You gotta admire that. And she—she simply appreciates a fellow entrepreneur."

And though he knew perfectly well what he wanted, Pops puzzled up his forehead and gazed down at the menu to signal this discussion was now *finito*.

"Well, her English is improving," said Stats, not sure what else he could say.

"Yeah," said Mark.

"Which reminds me of a story," said Pops.

Mark made a dramatic groan. "When does something not remind you of a story, Mr. Scientific?"

Pops shook his finger. "I tell them to you boys so you will not go stumbling out into this world completely ignorant of how things work."

They sat a moment while Angie set out the water, took everyone's order, then grabbed the menus and whisked away.

"We know, we know," said Mark, who loved to needle Pops, but also had a great sense of when to pull back.

"Anyways, your grandfather," Pops began, "had a hard time with English, too. Once I remember complaining about not being able to get a pair of these sneakers, Jumping Jacks, that all the other kids were wearing."

"Jumping Jacks?" Poor Mark could not resist.

"Hey." This time Pops sent him "the look." It froze Mark as Pops held him with magnum eyes, then followed with "the nod."

Mark lowered his head.

Order restored, Pops went on, allowing himself a smile.

"Anyways, I put all sorts of pressure on him. I gotta have these shoes, this and that. But you know, things were tight. Even so, I get to where I think I'm wearing the poor guy down, and he finally goes outside to talk it over with the neighborhood family, the other *paisanos* on the block there, to get some advice. So the next time I bring it up, how I had to have the Whiz Kids model Jumping Jacks because every one of my pals was wearing them, Papa comes back with, 'Markangelo, if everyone you know was going to jump off a boy named Cliff, what would you do?'"

Pops roared out a laugh at his own story. They all did. "That's what he said! *A boy named Cliff.* Papa, he didn't quite have the English down so good yet."

He laughed some more.

"Well, did you get the shoes or not?" Mark wondered.

"You know what, I never did. All I did was, at that moment, I tried not to laugh." He shook his head. "I tried my level best not to laugh, and I said, 'Papa, don't worry. I won't ever jump off of Cliff.' And that was that."

"Great story, Pops," said Mark, with a big smile. "I like to hear all that old-time stuff."

"Ah, geez, times, they are so different these days. But back then, you know, that's how it was."

That's how it is now, too, Stats wanted to say, for he sincerely believed it. Love is love. Honor is honor. And family is family, no matter who they are.

"Tell us another one, Pops. Tell us what it was like the first time you walked into Fenway Park."

Pulling back, Mark shot Stats a fierce-eyed glare, one that basically said, "That was probably the dumbest thing you could've asked."

Stats knew what Mark meant, since Pops no longer attended games, but he disagreed. He wanted Pops to reminisce, to remember the good times, the magic, and to one day actually come back and sit in his rightful place inside the ballpark he loved so much.

Pops brought his water glass close and took a sip. "Ah, you've heard that one before."

"Yeah, but not in a long time."

"Maybe later." He swiveled to look at the back of the room, toward the sound of the swinging kitchen door, and held his gaze until Angie appeared table side. Clearing a spot in the center, she set down a basket of warm breadsticks and an oval bowl of red sauce topped with fresh-grated Parmesan cheese.

They all dug in.

As Stats savored the chewy bread, he had an idea. "You know, Pops, I think this dough is strong enough for your chili dogs. You should talk to Angie about her recipe."

Mark agreed. "Yeah, really. What's a good hot dog bun, anyway, but a big fat breadstick?"

Angie reappeared with the entrees and began passing them out. "Who's making fun of my breadsticks?"

"Nobody!" said everybody, keeping their heads low.

"They're perfect," Pops added. "Someday, maybe I could get your recipe?"

She stood a moment, hands on hips, her dark eyes decoding him.

"All you have is to ask." She then reexamined the table. "All right. You boys, all set?"

Without waiting, she hastened off.

From out of left field, Pops said, "Reminds me a little of your mother."

He received two soft, uncertain hums in response.

Pops dabbed at his mouth with his red cloth napkin, then rested his fork and knife.

"I know I don't say too much about her."

Stats could feel Mark hunch over, tensing his arms. Neither boy dared look.

"But I should," Pops continued. "You boys need to grow up knowing about her, not wondering about her."

He re-clenched his knife and fork. He began to cut. "I've

been meaning to, you know, but . . ." He rested his hands, fork in the left, knife in the right. "What can you do?"

At that point, all three attacked their meals with vigor. They cut and stabbed and chewed and swallowed, working in a vacuum of silence, until two of them had cleaned their plates and the third had done his best, finishing up with a few last dabs of sauce and garlic bread.

Then, as if answering the question he'd left hanging, Pops said, "What I gotta do is take care of this bill collector situation first. Need to get that ironed out."

Mark rested his forearms on the table edge and sent Pops his own rendition of "the look."

"Whatever you decide, Pops, we're with you. It's a family matter. So whatever we need to do . . . we'll get it done."

That seemed to surprise Pops as much as it made him glow. He sat back and took them both in. Mark first, then Stats. With a grin and a huff, he reached over and grabbed each boy by the back of the neck and jostled them.

"I know we will," he said. "You are your mother's sons." He looked around again, as if for Angie, as if he suddenly needed to pay the bill.

"It's all taken care of, Pops," said Mark. "Remember?"

"Ah, geez." Pops waved a hand. After a quick sniffle, he slid from his seat and cleared his throat, coughing a bit louder than necessary.

"Okay, okay," he rasped. "Let's go. Game's coming on. I'll make the popcorn."

CHAPTER 25

The Sox went on to win three in a row against Minnesota and traded places with Toronto, climbing out of fourth by three percentage points. For one night. And on that night, Stats pretended he had been right all along. That maybe things do even out, given enough time.

It's logical. It's scientific. Things are turning around.

Then the Sox lost two in Kansas City to end their short road trip right back in fourth place—*and* both losses were directly linked to bad-luck runs. So much for turning anything around.

Meanwhile, Toronto had won three of four against Detroit, so the Sox slipped even deeper into fourth and were now eleven games out of first.

Stats could not ignore the trend. Yes, it was only the third week of June (lots of baseball to go), but on the other hand, it was only the third week of June (a long way to have fallen in just five weeks). On top of that, Billee had not pitched in seven days. Once again, after a poor performance, he had been passed over in the rotation.

• • •

On Wednesday, the first day the Sox were back in town, Billee showed up at the stand four hours before the start of the game. And he was pumped. It had been seven days since they'd seen each other and Stats was thrilled beyond words. For one thing, Billee had a plan!

"Here's the deal, Stat Man. We've got to get the hawks to come back to Fenway, right? But the question is, how? And the answer is right back there." He pointed to the rear of the stand.

Stats ducked under the counter and stepped to the other side, eager to see what his brilliant co-conspirator in curse-busting had come up with.

He followed Billee to the rear of the stand, where a small electric cart was parked, snugged up against the brick facade to the ballpark.

"We lure them back home," said Billee, "with what they need most." He stood next to a small mound on the cart's cargo area, which was covered with a green sheet. Then, like a stage magician, he yanked the sheet away.

"Ta-da!"

They both stood staring at a huge clutter of sticks, twigs, and leaves, all bundled together.

"What is that?" asked Stats.

"It's a bunch of sticks and stuff."

"You know, Billee, I actually do see what it is. What I meant was, what's it for?"

"A hawk's nest!" He bent over the bundle. "Don't you get it, bud? It's home sweet home. Hawks have excellent eyes, right?

So we put together a nest and set it out someplace. Before long, we got a couple of hawks living here. They tell their buddy hawks and bingo! The balance of nature is restored at Fenway."

Stats grinned widely. He loved the idea. "I always knew you were a genius," he said, "but this totally proves it. I kept thinking we had to litter the place with rats or catch the hawks and put them in cages or something. But this . . ." He walked from the front of the cart to the rear, examining Billee's sticks. "So where are we going to put the nest?"

"Well, that's what I want you to calculate out for us. It can't just be any old place. I've been reading about electromagnetic fields and the ancient pyramids, and—"

"Wait a minute. The pyramids? Electromagnetics? What's that have to do with a hawk's nest?"

"Not just the nest, Stat Man. The curse. People think a curse is bad luck. But it's not."

"It's not?"

"No, it's bad energy. It's all about the energy, bud. That's why we're bringing the hawks back."

"I thought it was to restore the natural balance."

"And natural balance is based on energy. That is, the flow of energy. Look, bud, the Chinese have known this for thousands of years. So have the Native Americans. And now Western scientists are finally proving what lots of cultures already knew. When your energy flows, all systems are go. You're golden!"

"You're starting to lose me."

"No worries. You asked, I answered." With a shrug, he set

a moccasined foot on the edge of the cart and re-examined his cluster of twigs.

"I asked, why pyramids. But now I'm not sure I want to hear . . ."

"Because"—Billee poked the air with his finger—"pyramids are energy magnets. That's why Cedro and Dusty and I wear crystal pyramids around our necks."

"You do?"

Billee shook open his medicine pouch. Out poured a few herbal stems, powdered leaves, and a miniature quartz pyramid, clear as glass.

"See?"

"Okay, but it doesn't seem to be doing you guys any good."

"Ah, bud, it can only do so much. But if we didn't have 'em, things would be a lot worse, believe me."

Stats could not dispute that, nor would he try. "Look, can we just get back to the hawk's nest? Where do we put it?"

Billee nodded. "That's what I'm getting at. It needs to be placed at the perfect spot to attract the highest degree of positive energy."

"I'm afraid to ask where that might be."

"I'm afraid I can't tell you. That's what I want you to figure out."

"How?"

"Easy breezy. What you have to keep in mind is this. The base of every four-sided pyramid, like the Great Pyramid at Giza, is a diamond."

Stats closed his eyes. "I'm going to yawn now."

"No, no, seriously. And Fenway Park already has a diamond. It's a ninety-foot square. So we know the baselines of our pyramid. Those are the baselines of our infield." He snapped his fingers. "Hey, maybe that's why they call it *base*ball!"

He paused a beat, then came back to earth. "Anyway, the Fenway pyramid is imaginary. I just need to know how high it is." He raised his palms to the sky. "Say it was built with the same proportions as the Great Pyramid at Giza, how high would it be? Okay? Find that out first. The nest should sit at the top of that pyramid along the most powerful ley line. So then research ley lines."

"Ley lines?"

"Energy lines. Look it up. You'll see. But once we have the line and the height, that's where we build the nest. Easy squeezy, double cheesy, buddy." He joggled the top of Stats's cap.

"Okay," said Stats as he straightened his hat. How could he say no? But first, he had to think. He loved a challenge. But he hated busywork. He'd have to check into Billee's plan to see if any of it made sense.

"Let me research the idea, okay? Might take a few days."

"Uh, no, Stat Man. No can do. I need that info ASAP. We have to build the nest *tonight*."

"Tonight? How come?"

"Because tonight's the summer solstice. And besides that, I'm pitching tomorrow."

"You are? But don't you think you should get your rest? We could get it done by your next start."

"Stat Man, the way things are going, I may not get another start. And look at Marichal, at Denton, at Woods. We're all struggling. Last year at this time, we were in a pennant race. This year, we're in the dungeon. Every single game counts. We need those hawks!"

Billee re-covered the sticks with the sheet. "Okay? So look, I'll pick you up in front of your house at midnight tonight."

"*Midnight?* What'll I tell Pops?"

"Oh, yeah." He thought a moment. "Why don't we get Marko to come with you?"

"Mark won't do it. He has a game tomorrow, too, and he sleeps, like, fourteen hours a night as it is."

"Okay, scratch Mark. Tell you what. You guys sleep on top of your roof sometimes, don't you? Why don't you do that to-night? Then just be ready to go out for a little midnight stroll. I'll have you back in no time. Besides, tonight is the summer solstice. It's gonna be magic! And we could use a little bit of magic."

Billee grinned with eyebrows arched.

What he could use, thought Stats, was a little bit of logic. But at the same time, he realized how much this meant to him. Besides, Stats loved the idea of a geometrical math challenge. He loved the idea of a late-night adventure at Fenway Park with the one and only Billee Orbitt. And, really, how long could it take to build a three-foot nest?

"Okay," he said. "I'll meet you at midnight."

CHAPTER **26**

At the first opportunity, Stats sent out a "data dump" request to the Stat Pack.

"Anything!" he wrote. "Need the magnetic power points of Fenway, ley lines, whatever. Need info on pyramids, dimensions, uses (why did they build them, anyways?), info on hawks' nests. Anything!"

Before long, Stats found himself sifting through his own personal Wikipedia of data on electromagnetic force fields in, on, around, and through Fenway Park.

Some he deemed useless. Some he flagged as significant. Mostly, it was a lot of reading.

Among the significant points, a few really stood out.

Hatonn, down in Louisville, wrote, "Most people believe the pyramids were built to be royal burial tombs. Not so. The first pyramids were built as healing stations. The Egyptians used strategically placed crystals to create positive healing energy in the heart of the pyramid."

That tied in to what Billee had said. Maybe they really were going to heal Fenway Park.

He also learned about ley lines from Willem Rike, a high school kid in New Hampshire.

"Ley lines," wrote Rike, "are intense rivers of energy within the earth. They usually connect two powerful or sacred sites."

Then Rike added something that floored Stats.

Dude, when it comes to pathways of energy, Boston is a hub. Think bike wheel. Boston = axle.

Turns out, Fenway Park connects two powerful and sacred sites. The ley line runs from center field right THRU home plate! It connects the oldest rocks on earth + newest rocks on earth. Isle of Iona + Island of Hawaii. Tons of chi if nothing blocks the flow. THIS is one MAJOR ley line.

L8r, sk8r

Stats could hardly believe this. A major energy line right through Fenway? But it took him only twelve minutes to verify what Rike had written.

In order to draw a straight line from the very mystical and sacred Isle of Iona, off the coast of Scotland, with its 4.5-billion-year-old surface rocks, all the way to the Kilauea Volcano on the Big Island of Hawaii, whose lake of fresh lava spills into the Pacific Ocean, where it cools and creates new rocky shoreline every day, your pencil would run right through Boston.

Once again, Stats could not wait to share everything he had discovered with Billee.

This, he loved.

Stats knew he would never experience the feeling of catching a deep fly ball up against the Green Monster or sending a home run over the right-field wall, but he reveled in that cool surge of energy he always felt when his brain was quick-flicking and his fingers were clicking.

For a kid like him, that would have to do.

Stats had almost fallen asleep when his eXfyle buzzed inside his sleeping bag. He got up and peered out over the edge of the half wall that ran along the roof of his house. Billee blinked his car lights from below.

Stats climbed down the old steel roof ladder to the back porch and eased softly onto the wooden deck. Then he tiptoed to the steps that led downstairs to the sidewalk.

Upon entering Billee's compact sports car, he said nothing, sinking low into the cushioned seat, shutting the door softly. As they pulled away, Billee asked, "What did you tell Pops?"

"I left a note. Said I'd be right back. But I hope he doesn't even read it."

"Where'd you put it?"

"On the roof."

"Dude," said Billee, but that was all he said.

"Where's that bunch of sticks?" asked Stats, looking around.

"In my locker. I buried it under my incognito wardrobe."

"Can you still get into the clubhouse and everything?"

"This late, usually not. But Paolo said he'd stick around so we could haul out the sticks, grab the cart, and go."

"So Paolo knows about this? Hey, maybe he can help."

"Not likely. He told me he'd be sleeping on his cot. He said, officially, he really doesn't want to know what we're up to."

"Oh." Stats peered up through his window over the rooftops. "Why is the summer solstice so special?"

"Because it's powerful. The sun's rays strike the earth head-on, sending us the maximum amount of solar energy for any day this year. And during the solstice, a bunch of planets line up with the earth and the sun forming one huge ley line. The first twenty-four hours are key. And it started tonight at 7:09."

"Which means?"

"Which means, we have the rest of tonight to get the nest in place. Then all day tomorrow it can absorb all this positive energy, which will not only help bring the hawks back and restore the natural balance, but if the nest is set in a real strong power point, it will completely negate the negativity of any curse in the Red Sox universe."

"Wow."

"Wow is right. That's why tonight's the night."

"You sure know a lot about this."

Billee grinned. "What else did you find out?"

Stats checked his eXfyle. "Carl Yastrzemski used to say that Fenway Park rejuvenated him after a road trip."

"True, so true."

"And there was a baseball commissioner named Giamatti who compared Fenway with the Great Pyramids at Giza. That goes along with what Yaz said, since I found out the first pyramid at Giza was built for healing."

Billee glanced over. "Good research, bud. Yaz had it right, too. Fenway can heal. I'd rank it right up there with the Mother Church here in Boston or the Dalai Lama's place in Tibet or the Hopi mesas in Arizona. All sacred. All timeless. And they all have what Fenway has."

Stats saw no reason to disagree.

Before long, the baseball cathedral was in view. Billee turned onto Lansdowne Street, which ran behind the Green Monster.

"Now tell me, where do we put the nest?"

"Well, I . . ."

"You figured it out, didn't you?"

"Sort of. My Stat Pack friend Willy Rike said that to do it right, we have to use the sacred geometry of baseball. That is, the circle, the triangle, and the diamond."

"Sounds about right."

"He says that in almost all ancient traditions, a circle represents the sun. A triangle represents heaven. A square, the earth. On a baseball field, there is one primary circle: the pitcher's mound."

"We can't build it there, bud."

"No, I know. Besides, a circle is not part of a pyramid. We need a triangle and a square."

"And the diamond is the square?"

"Right. And triangles are everywhere. Each base has one as a corner of the diamond. But one base is different."

"Home plate?"

"Right! And it's the strongest geometric shape of all. Here's what he said."

Stats brought up the text on his eXfyle and read. "'This symbol of the triangle upon the square originally came from off-planet sources.' So I wrote, 'Off-planet? UFO people? Ha ha.' And he says, yeah. Listen."

Affirmative. Google *The Law of One,* but not now.
Anyway, home plate's shape is formed by adding a
triangle to a square. Get it? Heaven on earth. In baseball
that lone spot on the diamond also represents the alpha
and the omega, the starting point on a runner's journey
as well as his ultimate destination. A real power point. So
let that be the cornerstone of your imaginary pyramid.

L8r, sk8r

"All right, dude," said Billee. "Great work. So, once again, where does the nest go?"

"In the stands, behind home plate."

Billee looked up, squinting.

"And," Stats continued, "the very tip of our imaginary pyramid would be about fifty-seven feet up, somewhere right around the catwalk just below the windows of the announcer's booth."

"Ah, just like we dreamed it."

"Pretty much." Stats looked down. "But since we can't build it there, I added fifty percent to all my calculations."

"Okay." After parking the car, Billee led Stats to a door on Van Ness that Stats had never seen before. Once inside, they set off down a dim hallway lit only by emergency lights. After reaching the concourse door at the other end, Billee headed off for the clubhouse to gather the sticks, while Stats made his way outside, climbing all the way to the top of the bleacher seats.

In a little while, Billee cruised out of a nearby tunnel, driving the cart right onto the upper deck promenade.

"Where do these go, Stat Man?" he called, indicating the bundle.

"Come here, I'll show you." He retrieved a laser pointer from his pocket.

After Billee walked up to join him, Stats pointed with his red beam. "Right there."

The beam hit the base of the flagpole at the very top of the old-fashioned stepped-roof facade that formed the front wall of the huge press box area overlooking the ballfield below.

"The only problem," said Stats, "is how to get on the roof."

"We'll use a rope. We'll have to start from down here. Somewhere."

That was when Stats noticed the twigs were bundled by a small piece of rope peeled off of a full coil holding maybe one hundred feet of line. Suddenly, he felt uneasy.

"What do you mean, *we*?" he asked. "You're the only one going up, right?"

"Oh, sorry, bud. No, I didn't mean 'we.' I meant you."

"*Me?* Billee, are you—" He stopped short of asking the obvious question. "How am I supposed to get way up on top of that roof? You know I'm just a kid, right?"

"Sure. And that's what makes you just the right size to hoist up nice and easy-like. We'll toss a rope over a beam or something above the stands, then I'll pull you up to the edge of the roof. You toss the bundle over and climb on. Set up the nest, and I'll lower you down."

Stats stared at the flagpole. "Billee, I'm not getting the picture. How do I actually climb on?"

"Don't worry. I'll rig you a harness with a step about waist high. I saw it once on a survivor-in-the-rain-forest show. Seriously. When you get close enough, you'll . . . uh, you'll figure it out."

"I will?" He *seriously* doubted it.

Billee avoided any hint of eye contact. "Sure."

"Don't you think maybe *we* should think this thing through a little more?"

"I do, I do," said Billee as he began unraveling the rope. "No, you're right." Using a seat back as a form for shaping, he started designing the rope seat. "That's exactly what I want you to be thinking about while I figure out the harness and hoist."

Billee had a great arm. An obvious observation, Stats knew, but to see him throw a weighted batting doughnut tied to the end of a rope up into the rafters was unbelievable. He threaded two needles, one on the way up—between two support beams—and one at the edge of the roof itself as the weight skidded just over another support arm, falling cleanly to the other side, and dangling there until he let out more slack.

"We'll have you up and down before you know it, Stat Man." The heavy doughnut-on-a-rope glided back down into Billee's waiting hand. He removed the weight and attached the small seat he had created, the type you might see a rock climber use.

Stats stood back and eyed the rope. "It's kind of thin, isn't it?"

"Hey, no worries. It'll hold five hundred pounds. Said so on the wrapper. Now, look, I'll strap you in, clip on the bundle, and hoist you right up. When you get to the top, toss the bundle up first. Then climb onto the harness here." He pointed to the seat.

"How do I do that?"

"It won't be that hard. I'll talk you through it."

"Talk me through it?" Stats took the mountaineering seat from him and squeezed his eyes shut.

While Billee fussed with the sticks, Stats pulled in two deep breaths, hoping to bring more oxygen into his brain. Gripping the rope near his face, he gave one last big exhalation.

Then he softly added, "I want to know how you ever talked me into this."

CHAPTER **27**

Billee kept his focus on the mission. With a quick snap, he clipped the bundle of sticks to Stats's belt.

"Once you're on the roof, bud, you just walk over to the flagpole, build the nest, and then I lower you back down. Voom! Voom! Piece of cake."

Billy hoisted away. Slowly Stats began to rise. He had counted on going up. He had not counted on swinging from side to side. And the twirling-like-a-ballerina part that came next was completely unexpected.

About halfway up he was spinning and swinging so wildly, he had to tell Billee to stop.

"I'm getting dizzy."

"Okay, just grab my line. Here, I'll bring it closer. Grab it and stabilize yourself."

It took a while for Stats to even locate the hoisting rope Billee had brought over to him. As he spun past, he wrapped his forearm into it and finally came to a stop.

"Sorry, bud. I didn't know you were going to spin."

"Look, maybe you better lower me down. It doesn't really seem like this is going to work."

"Sure, it is, Stat Man. You're halfway up."

"Then I'm also halfway down. See my point?"

Billee ignored the question. "Look, let my line slip through your arms as I pull you up. That'll help stabilize you. Plus, the higher you go, the less you'll swing. Just don't look down."

"Don't worry." Stats again shut his eyes. He felt himself rising.

"Just another five feet," said Billee. By the sound of Billee's voice, Stats figured he must be walking the line back instead of wrapping it around something. Stats preferred a nice solid wrap. What if the rope slipped out of Billee's hands? That doughnut had fallen in a *hurry*.

At the very moment of that thought, Stats suddenly dropped a good ten feet before Billee managed to stop his fall.

"What are you *doing*?" Stats screamed, his voice cracking. "Trying to kill me?"

"Sorry. I slipped. Won't happen again. But I had the rope the whole time, so no worries. I was looking up, and there was a big wet spot down here, so . . ."

Stats squeezed his eyes even tighter. Great, he thought. Nice image. One more slip like that, and there'll be *two* big wet spots down there.

"Well, be careful."

"I got you, bud."

Finally Stats rose up near enough that he could almost touch the edge of the grandstand roof. Almost.

"I can't reach it."

"Can you stretch?"

"Can you fly? Look, I'm only four-foot-six, and *that's* on my tiptoes. I'm at least a foot away."

"Okay, okay." Billee took a moment before he spoke again. "All right, Stat Man, listen. I'm going to lower you down."

Finally. Mission unaccomplished, and he did not care. Yes, he truly wanted to lure the hawks back, he truly wanted to restore balance to Fenway Park. But this might be the dumbest thing he had ever done in his life, eclipsing even the time he rode down Beacon Street on a bike with no brakes. But at least on the bike he could drag his feet. From here he could touch nothing but nothing.

Stats began to descend. Then stopped. "What's the matter?" he asked.

"That's far enough. Now you can start to rock back and forth until you swing up high enough to grab the catwalk. From there I think you can toss the sticks onto the roof."

"Are you nuts?"

Billee gave a one-legged stomp, jerking his head forward. "Why do people keep asking me that? No, I think this'll work."

"Then why don't *you* come up and try it?"

"Believe me, bud. If I could, I would. Just give me your best shot."

So he shot. He swung out a little, back a little. Out, then

back. Each time Stats passed through the middle of his arc, his stomach flipped.

"You're almost there," called Billee. "One more big kick."

Stats gave it all he had. It was now or never. As he swung toward the press box area, he kicked his feet out for an extra lunge.

They touched! His feet actually kissed the metal catwalk below the windows. Then he swooped back the other way and lost virtually all of his momentum, except for that stupid twirl.

"It's no use," he said. "I can't get close enough, and even if I did, I'm not strong enough to grab on and pull myself up. Billee, you have to do this."

This time Billee did not respond, but Stats noticed right away he was sliding down toward ground zero. When his toes touched concrete, his knees collapsed.

Billee had to catch him and steady him up.

"Okay, buddy. No worries. We'll figure something out."

At just hearing the tone in Billee's voice, Stats felt crushed. He had promised his hero something and had let him down. He looked back up at the target spot. It did not seem all that high from down here.

Could he try it again? Could he somehow figure out a better approach?

"What about this, Billee? What if you lift me back up, and I swing back and forth from just underneath the lip? I bet I could swing the bundle onto the roof from there."

Billee tilted his head back. "I don't think that's gonna work either."

Stats had never heard Billee sound so defeated.

"Look, Stat Man, I'm sorry I got you into all this."

"No, it's okay."

"Believe me, if I could do it myself, I would. It's just that I can't go up there either. I'm, uh, I'm nervous about heights."

What?

"How can *you* be nervous about anything? Last year you shut out the Yankees in Yankee Stadium!"

Then, in that same instant, Stats recalled how Billee had gone so slowly and carefully up the ladder onto Stats's roof to see the batting cage.

Now he felt even worse. So Billee Orbitt was afraid of heights. How could anyone have guessed that?

Deciding he could not bear to let his friend down, Stats said, "Billee, I want to try one last time. Come on, let's hit it with our best shot."

Billee grinned at the line.

"No, really," said Stats.

"Think so, huh?" Billee peered up at the challenge. "Okay, look, I do have another idea. Sort of a backup deal I thought of at the last minute."

He winked at Stats, who smiled. He should've known he could always count on Billee to have a backup plan.

Billee waved. "Follow me."

They returned to the electric cart at the upper-deck tunnel mouth. Billee tugged on an old frazzled tarp and pulled it off the cargo area. Underneath were four huge metal cylinders and a shiny roll of silver duct tape.

"What's in the tanks?" asked Stats.

"Helium."

"Where'd they come from?"

"Paolo was filling balloons when I saw him this afternoon. You know, for the show Saturday night."

"So what's your plan?"

Billee snapped open a toolbox built into the side of the cart under the bed. He pulled out an uninflated beach ball.

"What do we do?" asked Stats. "Float the sticks up there with helium balloons?" He was beginning to like this.

"That's what I was thinking." Billee knelt down and pulled out an armload of deflated beach balls. "Paolo's got a ton of these."

Now Stats finally knew what happened to all of those beach balls the crowds slapped around before the security guys confiscated them.

Then Billee looked him in the eye. "But I've actually got an even better idea."

CHAPTER 28

It took a while for Stats to google up the information he needed to determine whether the four tanks held enough helium to lift a person into the air.

The answer was yes and no. It seemed as if there was enough helium to float someone off the ground, but not just anyone. The guy could weigh no more than thirty-three kilos.

"How much is that in American?" asked Billee.

Stats had only a moment to get himself out of one more loony situation. All he had to do was answer, "Oh, it's about forty pounds."

Instead, he spoke from his heart.

"It's, like, seventy-two pounds."

Billee nodded. He smacked his lips open, took in a breath, and let it right out. He did not even bother to ask his next question out loud. He simply looked at Stats and raised both eyebrows.

"Um," said Stats, "I weigh about sixty-five pounds."

Billee nodded again. He began to fill the plastic balls.

As Billee worked, Stats folded himself into the driver's seat of the cart and silently watched the constellation Pegasus, which had appeared over the rooftops along the third base line. After a while, he realized the flying horse was joining them as the lead star, Enif, which was Arab for "the horse's nose," slowly but surely began heading east across the center of the sky dome.

"Pegasus," Stats announced finally, without even looking at Billee. "Coming this way."

Billee stopped what he was doing to gaze west. "I wonder when it'll sit right smack-dab above us?"

"Don't know. I'll look it up."

Stats searched his favorite star site for the Boston sky data. "Well, this table's not that precise. Let me zero in." He quickly entered the exact longitude and latitude coordinates for Fenway Park in relation to when Enif would top the diamond dome.

Whoa. He could hardly believe his result.

"Hey, Billee. I got the exact time for the moment Pegasus is right over Fenway."

"Good, read it off."

"You're not going to believe this." He looked up to catch Billee's eyes.

Billee lifted his chin, then he raised his eyebrows in a silent question.

Stats replied, "Four-oh-six."

Magical numbers to any baseball aficionado, let alone a Red Sox fan, they represented the batting average of one Ted

Williams, who in 1941 became the first man since 1930, and the last man ever, to hit over .400 in a single season.

Billee hooted as he spun the helium valve wide open, restarting his task with a grin. "Believe in magic, bud?"

"I do now."

It took twenty-seven beach balls of assorted sizes, colors, and designs to empty the tanks. Working together, Stats and Billee bundled the various balls into duct-taped groups of four. Then they tied all seven bundles together into one huge bouquet anchored to the top rail of the upper-deck walkway.

After undoing the anchor rope and wrapping it around his waist, Billee decided to take the flying beach balls out for a spin.

"Well," he said, "here goes nut thing!" And off he went. The pull of the rig was so strong, Billee could gambol around the upper-deck promenade with long loping strides, like an astronaut bouncing on the moon.

He came leap-jogging back, laughing.

"Well, are you ready?"

CHAPTER **29**

From that moment, the night took on a magical glow.

The low glimmer of light inside Fenway seemed to golden up and began pulsating everywhere Stats looked. At the moment of his own liftoff, he felt an instant kinship with every bird that had ever flown within the walls of this ancient fortress.

He would later describe the electric surge that charged through his bones as a hawkness, though he would also admit he hardly knew what that word meant. It just felt right.

His eyes focused in crystal clarity. His breath flowed high into his chest. He laid one sure hand on his bundle of sticks, gripped the tether line with the other, and up he rose.

Ten feet, twenty, thirty. Floating straight up, a boy on a cloud on a top-secret mission, he seemed to have become a human lightning rod for every unanswered dreambolt prayer sent skyward in the history of this sacred slice of land.

He could sense them all, back to the days of Tris Speaker,

Babe Ruth, and Joe Cronin. Through the days of Jimmy Foxx, Ted Williams, and Bobby Doerr. And forward to the days of Johnny Damon, Roger Clemens, and Manny Ramirez. He heard their thoughts.

Yes, the whispered prayers of big-league ballplayers whistled around him as he rose.

With a fierceness and finesse he had never known, but was now so strangely his own, Stats tossed the bundle of hawk's nest makings onto the press box rooftop, behind its half-wall facade.

Then he fastened the tether line to a small crosspiece on the shiny new flagpole atop the wall's peak to hold the balloons in place while he dropped from the rope seat onto the roof.

Once he could walk upon the rooftop, he pulled out his eXfyle and found the illustrations of a hawk's nest that he had saved for reference. Using the same layered weaving shown in the drawings, he constructed the best replica of a natural hawk's home he could.

As a final touch, he added some shredded wool socks he'd cut up in his room and stuffed into his pockets. Red socks. Using the woolen shreds, he layered and cushioned the floor of the nest as if it were a royal throne. He took three pictures and stepped back into his seat. Before he unhitched the beach balls to ride them down again, Stats took a moment to gaze out across the Boston skyline, eerily unhindered by the ballpark lights.

But nothing he saw in any direction—the new Hancock

Tower, the Prudential Tower, and the R2-D2 building on Huntington Avenue—compared, in beauty or grace, with the architecture of the building he stood upon.

Which was as it should be, as far as Stats was concerned, for no occupation practiced within any of those landmark structures could compare in skill or complexity or worth to the high artwork of those men who had declared somewhere in their Olympian boyhoods the intention to dedicate their lives to mastering a child's game. And to never give up.

"Got it?" yelled Billee.

"Got it!" Stats replied. "Beam me down, Billee."

In the next moment he was gliding his way toward Boston's unluckiest pitcher, whose muscular arms easily reeled him in, coiling the line around two metal rails. All in all, his trip into the heights of heaven had taken less than fifteen minutes. And now he was back to the mortal realm with, he hoped, the gratitude of a rebalanced bio-system, if not a pocketful of luck.

But he was not done yet. Just as his feet touched the top of the upper deck rail, he said, "Billee, do you think you could take me down to the field?"

"You mean fly you there?" Billee sent a thoughtful glance toward first base below. Without any further hesitation, he said, "Wrap your legs through the railing and just hang tight for a minute."

Stats did as he was instructed.

Billee freed the coil of rope and tossed it all the way down to the field-level seats.

"Don't let go until I tell you to, bud, or we'll have to call Logan to shoot you down." He winked, then headed for the tunnel.

Stats wrapped his arms through the bars as well, and hung tight.

In a few minutes, Billee had reappeared below and gathered up the coil of rope.

"Hold on!" he called. "Don't let go just yet."

He hopped over the wall and onto the field, then spun around, wrapping his own body with the line.

"Okay, *now!*" he called, waving his hat from the first-base media pit.

Stats untangled himself from the upper-deck rail and let go.

Instantly Billee began flying him like a kite. The weight of the rope between the two was enough to keep Stats from floating too high—until Billee reeled him closer.

Pulling him over the Red Sox dugout and onto the field, Billee brought Stats along until he hovered directly above him. Then he let out more line, sending the flying boy some thirty feet above the grass.

Stats could feel the pulse of his heart in his stomach, in his shoulders, hands, and legs. Or was it the pulse of Fenway taking over his body and soul?

For as he floated in the night, Stats realized his heart had never felt so weightless, so normal. It was beating free and easy. Like hawk wings through the sky.

This fact might have surprised a normal boy, one who lived

for the booming adrenaline rush that this sort of event would supply. But Stats felt nothing beyond an elevated calm.

And then he realized why. Fenway Park had always been a part of his heart. A normal part.

Unless a kid had grown up right outside these brick walls, unless he had been guided through the high holy gates at an early age, down the green serpentine walkways to the narrow weathered-gray wood-slat seats Stats could still recall from his first-ever baseball game, he could not hold in his heart the pulsings of this hundred-year-old park the way Stats could.

Obviously, a kid might come close. Why? Because every clumpy crabgrass ballfield in every small town across the land, with its foot-carved riverine base paths, its dented-metal Coca-Cola scoreboard, its rock-clay pitcher's mound, had a bit of Fenway in it. Every dusty city dugout made of concrete blocks with splintered wood benches was made from particles of Fenway. Every empty city sandlot, every playground ballfield Stats had walked past in all of his long short years held a bit of Fenway, in the same way every teardrop holds a part of the sea.

That's because Fenway was more than an exact place. It was the love of baseball itself. It was the wobbly knees of a first at bat. It was the full gut tingle, the utter exultation that shakes through a small boy's vernal bones when, for the very first time, a ball thrown by his brother jars the pocket of his glove and stays in place.

Fenway Park is all these things to all boys, all girls, all across the globe.

"Take me over the mound, Billee."

Slowly Stats glided over the chalk, onto the infield, and hovered above Billee, standing on the pitcher's mound.

"Hey, watch this!" Stats yelled. Wrapping his right foot around the tether, he stuck his left leg out in front of him, high into the air.

"I'm Luis Tiant!"

"You're the spittin' image," said Billee.

Stats laughed in glee. He leaned forward to ask, "Hey, can we go to the outfield? I want to play one off the Green Monster."

Again, he was bounding through space, whizzing off to his personal Emerald City.

Approaching deep left, Stats began to call the play. "Top of the ninth, folks. Last chance for the Cardinals."

Billee brought him to the wall.

"Get ready to bounce me off it, Billee."

"Coming right up."

Stats looked back toward home plate. "Long fly ball to left, folks. Oh, boy, he got it all. It's gonna be trouble. Yastrzemski's back. He's looking up . . ."

At that point, Billee pulled down on the rope a good five feet.

". . . He might have a chance. He jumps!"

Billee let out the slack just as Stats reached high and leaped toward the sky, and the pack of beach balls slammed into the thirty-seven-foot wall, bouncing their way up and over it, and Stats along with them.

"Yastrzemski crashes into the scoreboard, folks . . ."

Atop the rim of the monstrous wall, Stats held his glove hand at full extension.

"And he *makes the catch!* Holy guacamole! Alfredo Carl 'Yaz' Pagano makes an incredible catch! And the Boston Red Sox win the 1967 World Series!"

"Woo-hoo!" shouted Billee. "Nice grab, Yaz. You haven't lost a thing."

They laughed and they bounced all around the park, circling the outfield, then the bases.

"Freddy Ballgame, folks, whacks another one, a massive shot, over the right-field wall. What a blast! I tell you, it looked like a spaceship zooming over Williamsburg!"

Stats had never felt so elated in all his life. He had never "run" so fast or "jumped" so high. Had never laughed so hard.

So this is baseball, he thought.

Wow, what a game.

CHAPTER **30**

"Billee?" asked Stats as he sat gazing into the stars from his balloon seat, still hovering twenty feet above his friend anchored upon home plate. "If you weren't a Major League Baseball pitcher, what would you be?"

And though Billee had been meditating for the past half hour, he responded rather quickly. "Oh, a thousand things, buddy. I could live ten lifetimes and never do all the things I'd like to do."

"Like what?" Stats could not even dream of a dream bigger than the one Billee was living.

"One thing I always wanted to do was to just travel the earth, to vagabond around it, say, ten or fifteen times, to see all I can see. I'd head south to start with. Venezuela, Colombia, Patagonia."

"I never would have guessed that." But now, somehow, he could understand. If you felt that you had been "dropped" upon a foreign planet, as Billee said he did, the least you could do was to explore the place and find out what all it had to offer.

"Yep, I want to see every place I can." Billee paused to think again. "Long-haul trucking. *That's* something I'd like to try someday. Eighteen-wheeling from coast to coast. Also like to be a mountain climber. Someday I want to climb the face of El Capitan out there in Yosemite National Park."

Stats looked down at the eXfyle he clutched in his palm. "Let me see." He quickly had images of climbers on El Cap's south wall and a video clip shot from halfway up.

"Whoa. Billee! It's a million miles high."

"It's huge."

"I don't think I could ever do that."

"Well, you know, I say this: If you decide you want to do something and you can see yourself doing it, then I believe you can. And I mean anything."

Stats looked up from the screen, imagining he had decided to climb the sheer granite walls of El Capitan, straight up, over a mile high. In his mind, he was a pretty good climber.

"Maybe," he said, memorizing the image. "Maybe I could, too, someday. Maybe after I learn how to ride a skateboard."

Maybe, he thought, after my operation.

Billee sat quietly, knees bent, his legs crossed at the shins, not bothering to add anything more.

Stats appreciated the way Billee could let an idea sit there on its own and not ruin it with words. Quieting the mind, he had called it.

Then Stats remembered something. "But I thought you didn't like heights."

"I don't. And that's why. Maybe if I could climb a giant rock wall, like El Cap, I'd be okay after that."

Again, Stats sat back and pondered. Imagine, with all Billee's done in his life, he still thinks about the things he can't do. And he still plans to get them done. Just to be "okay after that."

Stats tried to remember what Mark had done with his old skateboard.

This, he promised himself, would not be his last exciting ride.

He leaned back and stared directly at Pegasus as it reared up into the sky, ready for liftoff, and he now knew for certain nothing would ever be the same again. A new era had begun.

At about 3:45 A.M., in the still morning calm, Stats peered down over his shoes to check on Billee, who sat below, still, as he put it, gathering the energy of the solstice. Stats had spent the last hour or so trying to absorb all that had happened to him on this mystical night. And why. Finally, he felt courageous enough to ask a certain question he could not seem to shake.

"Billee?" he began.

"Yeah, bud?"

"Why did you choose to be my friend?"

"What?"

"Was it because—you know, because I'm so small and everything, and you thought—"

Billee leaned back to look straight up. "Stop right there, Stat

Man. Stop." He waved his hand. "Because I see where you're going. What, the big-league pitcher felt sorry for the little guy and blah, blah, blah? Look, not even close. For one thing, you're an incredible kid. Okay?" He shook his finger at Stats for emphasis. "I knew that the first time I stepped up to the stand, and you were all business. You started my order and didn't bat an eye. Even though I was this kooky celebrity, this Major League ballplayer, you saw me as a regular guy who simply wanted a hot dog and who deserved to be treated with equal respect to all the other hot-dog-wanters standing there in line."

Now Billee lowered his gaze and spoke to the pitcher's mound. "And as I got to know you, even though I could tell you were a boy genius, I saw you as a regular guy, too, who only wanted to make me a decent hot dog. Which I respect. I tip my hat to you, to Mark, and to Pops. You're my kind of people. So it wasn't so much me choosing you. I was honored that you chose me, to treat me as an equal." He put his palms upon his knees and now seemed to be addressing the outfield, addressing Fenway Park itself. "That's all I ever ask of anyone, but you'd be surprised at how few people actually do that."

Stats, however, was not surprised at all. To him, the surprising thing was how he understood perfectly what Billee had just said. He wanted people to see him as normal.

"Oh. Okay. I was just wondering."

They both retreated to silence. It was the happiest silence Stats had ever felt.

Maybe Stats could have had a conversation like this in a

normal setting, with Billee on the bull pen bench, say, or at the hot dog stand. But he seriously doubted it.

It took this. It took flying in the sky over Fenway Park, over a power point, along ancient ley lines, on the summer solstice, for a kid like him and the wildest man in baseball to rise above the everyday chitchat and have the first real man-to-man talk he'd ever had.

Now, that was balance.

CHAPTER 31

In the early morning of June 21, 2012, Billee eased his car through the streets of South Boston.

Within a few minutes, they arrived at the curb in front of the sixty-five-year-old two-story building Stats called home. Stars still twinkled, but dawn was closing in fast.

"Get some sleep," said Billee, pulling to a stop.

"You too." Stats opened the door and stepped out.

"Ah, don't worry. Me and the Babe, we keep the same hours."

Stats smiled, knowing that besides being a hefty hot dog eater, Babe Ruth had also been quite a night owl and, even so, had done all right for himself. He quietly pushed the door shut and started to leave. Then he stopped himself and turned.

"Billee?" He leaned down to the window. "Thanks a lot for inviting me to come along. It was really fun."

"You bet, bud." He jutted his chin. "Hey. You know what I hope?"

"No, what do you hope?"

"I hope we're friends for a long time."

A long time? Stats wished that one moment could have lasted for infinity. He wished he could have said something spectacular, too, but everything he could think of saying was beyond words.

They nodded, and that was it. Two desperadoes bidding each other adios after the ride of a lifetime.

The everyday go-to-work world, which was just beginning to stir, would never understand what they had just gone and done. But they did.

Tonight, they had tipped their hats to the universe. And now all they had left to do was to go about their business and wait for the universe to tip back.

CHAPTER 32

At 7:05 Thursday night, Billee completed his final warm-up toss, and everyone around section 71 sat poised for a great game.

"Tonight's the night," said Lucy to no one in particular. "I can feel it."

Behind her, Mr. McCord asked, "What do you feel, Lucille?"

Lucy turned and waved her rolled-up program. "Tonight, everyone hits. Everyone runs. Everyone scores."

"I feel that way, too," said Mrs. McCord. "But it's more than a feeling."

"More than a feeling?" Her husband looked around for consensus. "You mean the merry fans walk away winners tonight?"

"I mean," said Lucy, "the merry Sox walk away winners tonight."

Mark nudged Stats. "Hope she means *Red* Sox."

Point taken. The Chicago *White* Sox were in town for a short two-game series, and having beaten the Boston Red Sox last night, they were riding a three-game winning streak and sitting all alone in second place in the Central Division.

But Billee moved with an air of confidence Stats had only now realized he'd been missing over his last several starts. Billee stood on the mound, looked in, and got his sign from Burly Fiske. He nodded. He pitched.

Fastball. Ninety-six miles an hour. Strike one. Everybody cheered.

They cheered again when he retired the Chicago leadoff man on four pitches, finishing the poor guy with his buckler, in at the knees.

Stats looked into the sky. There must be a hawk up there somewhere, he figured. He glanced toward the scorebooth. Nothing. Maybe they were already settled into their new home.

Or maybe not.

Billee would go on to face seven more batters that inning. He would retire none. The whistles and cheers came no more. After the third walk of the inning, two with the bases loaded, Billee was gone.

What *happened*? thought Stats. Everything was supposed to be so perfect after such an amazing night. Was it just too soon to expect anything to have changed? Or, worse yet, could it have all been for nothing?

While watching reliever Kurt Pfenning chill the White Sox, fanning his first hitter and getting ahead on the next guy, Stats noticed the pitcher casually rotate his right shoe a few times, as if loosening his ankle.

After two more pitches, Coach Stallings jumped out onto the field, asked for time, and conferenced with Pfenning. Immediately, the coach waved for the trainer.

Pfenning would not throw another pitch.

"What happened?" asked Stats.

"He landed wrong," said Mark. "It was four pitches ago. I remember seeing him hop a little after throwing a changeup. Didn't seem right."

It wasn't. Pfenning left the game, and the carnage resumed.

What followed was a long game, as the Red Sox went through five pitchers on the night. What followed for Stats and Mark was a long, quiet bus ride home. Mark was eager to get to bed. Stats was eager to get free of a weird feeling that had crept into his mind. Before he turned out the light, Stats checked a few of the blogs, just to see how Red Sox Nation was reacting.

Most were convinced that Billee needed to be sent down to Pawtucket to work out his kinks. No, thought Stats. Don't send him away. We need him. Some fans argued for a bull pen stay, letting Billee pitch only in the middle innings of games that didn't matter. A mop-up guy. And those were the friendly ones.

In the morning, Stats checked again. He had awoken with the same feeling he had retired with. That Billee was going away. And he was right.

The Sox were sending Billee to Pawtucket for a "rehabilitative" stay. Stats knew what that meant. If he could not regain his form, he would be gone. Out of baseball. History.

He realized then, it *had* all been for nothing.

CHAPTER 33

"Hey there, good to see you, Mr. Lucchesi," said Pops as he spotted the Boston Red Sox president the next day approaching the stand. "Step right on over here. I'll give you personal service."

Mr. Lucchesi, thought Stats. Maybe I can find out what his plans are for Billee. What if the Sox don't ever want him back? Were they thinking about trading him to another club?

"That's what I like about this place, Pops. Plenty of personal service by the family who knows what they're doing."

"Been doing it so long, the chili dogs are starting to follow us home." He barked out a laugh and tapped the grill to clean his tongs. "What can I do for you?"

"I wonder if I could speak to Freddy for a minute."

"Absolutely." He turned. "Alfredo, Mr. Lucchesi wants a word."

Stats had heard the whole thing, but had only just then looked up, pretending to be quite busy. "Sure, be right there." He gave the chili kettle another stir.

Pops winked at the Red Sox chief exec. "Can't rush magic, eh?"

The club president understood completely. "I haven't been able to yet, Pops."

Stats wiped his hands on his apron and stepped over behind Pops at his station. "Hello, sir."

"Hello, Freddy. I want to ask you something. The video production people thought it might be fun for you to give your little speech during a game instead of taping it ahead of time. What do you think?"

Stats shrugged. "I don't know. Might not be as good if I don't get a chance to rehearse it in front of the cameras a few times first."

"Well, that's part of the idea. We don't want a slick production from you. You're the fan of the future. You love the game. You're loyal. Your family has a long history of being associated with Fenway Park. We thought it might be nice if you told us what you like about being here. No rigmarole. No script. Just something short and sweet from a true young fan. What do you say?"

"I like the 'short' part."

The man laughed. "Don't blame you. Twenty, thirty seconds tops. We think you'll be great. Half the crowd knows you and your family anyway from all the years you've been down here. It'll be a real treat for everybody."

Oh, man, thought Stats. If only he knew those days may soon be over, that Pops is on the verge of selling the stand, just so we can afford to pay our bills. Still, Stats had to try. Billee would want him to.

"Okay, I can probably do that."

"Super." He rubbed his hands together. "What about tomorrow night? With the Yankees in town, it'll be a good crowd. Saturdays, we usually get a lot of kids coming out."

"Sure, I guess."

Tomorrow! During the Yankees series? With Billee in Pawtucket?

But what could he say? "Uh, could I ask one thing? How long do you think Billee will be gone?"

Mr. Lucchesi scratched at the gray stubble on his jawline. "Can't say, Freddy. I want him back up here as much as anyone. We'll give him a few starts in Paw and see how it goes."

Stats nodded. "Hope it goes good."

"As do I." He stepped back. "Okay, all set?"

Stats gave another nod.

"Super, super." He turned. "Pops, a star is born. The kid's a natural."

"He's a bright boy," said Pops. "He'll do all right by you."

The man thanked Stats and Pops and left.

"You think so, Pops?" he asked.

"Of course. You're gonna knock 'em out. You'll be terrific."

"No, I mean what you said about being bright."

Pops gentled his eyes. "Ah, Alfredo. You're the brains of this whole family." He spoke louder. "You're so brilliant you make us all shine just hanging around you. Ain't that right, Markangelo?"

Mark turned from the customer he was helping to shout out one of his plays on words. "You got that bright!" He went back to work.

And that was that.

All Stats and his bright brain had to worry about now was thinking up something brilliant to say.

Stats decided to study the Fen-Cent message delivered during Friday night's game, looking for clues. Unfortunately, it turned out to be a "slick production"—just the opposite of what he would do.

Two Boston singers, Kay Hanley, dressed in old-fashioned dance hall clothes from the 1920s, and Amanda Palmer, dressed basically in old-fashioned underwear, teamed up to perform their Red Sox tribute called "The Knights of Fenway."

> Every night the Knights of Fenway
> Segue into my soul
> Every night they tend to send me
> Someplace outside control
>
> My all-time heroes are a couple of Bill-os
> Who remind myself of me
> One of them's named Buckner
> The other one's name is Lee

Mark could not tear his eyes away. It was fancy. It was dancey. "See, Freddy, that's all you gotta do."

"Wear skimpy clothes and shake a lot?"

"No, just talk from your heart. Personal stuff. How much you like coming to the park, hanging out with Billee Orbitt, snagging foul balls during the game."

"You always get the foul balls. I've never caught one."

"Yeah, but you're excited when I glove it, aren't you? And tell 'em how you always keep score. People eat that stuff up."

"Really?" That sparked an idea. "Maybe they'd let me announce one batter's entire at bat, pitch by pitch. That would be awesome."

"That won't happen. But look at it this way. Your whole message will be a baseball broadcast. It's like a dream come true, Stat Man."

Stats smiled at Mark. No one but Billee had ever called him that. But now Billee was gone.

On one point, however, Mark was right. It *was* a chance in a lifetime to speak to the crowd at Fenway. Even for twenty seconds.

But what in the world was he going to say?

CHAPTER **34**

At least there existed one aspect of Stats's life where good news prevailed. It was the only bit of hope he had to hold on to, that maybe something in his life might turn out all right. As of today, Saturday, June 23, 2012, out of all YMBL shortstops in North America, Mark Pagano's numbers were the best. Only one game to go.

"Congrats, dude," said Jacky as Mark and Stats arrived in Stonybrook for the ten o'clock game.

"Way to go, Mark." Sully Frankson slapped his hand.

The congratulations came from everyone on the team, leaving Mark a little out of sync and the last one ready to take the field for warm-ups. As he hurried to lace up his cleats, Coach Carrigan sat down alongside him on the bench. Stats rustled through some pages and pretended not to be listening.

"I've seen all the numbers, Mark," the coach said. "Looks like you're a shoo-in for this thing. Chance of a lifetime."

"I know. It's hard to believe."

"How do you feel?"

"Good, good. A little nervous about it, but good."

"Yeah." The coach let the word hang there a moment before adding, "I was thinking, why don't you enjoy the feeling a little and sit this one out?"

"What do you mean?" asked Mark.

"Well, there's still today. What if you get a few bad hops out there? What if you go oh-for-four? The thing is, there's no one else for you to catch. You can only go downhill from here."

Stats bent over the scorebook, coughing softly to kick-start his heart.

Coach Carrigan shook Mark's knee. "Take a breather. That way, you're in for sure."

"I could do that? I mean, just not play?"

"This game doesn't mean anything. We're in first place. The Stallions are in fourth. The only difference today's game might make is to slide you backward. You could lose your spot. Am I right, Stats?"

Stats pretended to be caught by surprise, taking a moment to glance up. Then he slid down the bench with his nose in the scorebook. "Well, technically, I guess. One error in the field would drop him to .995. Same as this other guy." He pointed to a name. "Two errors would not be good at all. That would let a couple of better hitters gain ground in fielding, and they could close in if they have good days at the plate. But if Mark even goes one-for-three, one error wouldn't matter too much. Overall, he'd still be ahead. Unless, like I say, one of these guys has a great day, and Mark has a really bad one."

Mark sniffed a sharp breath and gazed out toward center

ndulated as he pondered the matter. Then they
hawked out a load of spit toward the chalk line.

I go one-for-four?"

ats calculated. "If you do that and this guy in L.A. goes
nree-for-four, he'd edge you out by a couple of points."

"Up to you," said Coach Carrigan. "But you pretty much got
a sure thing here. Rather sit down, breathe easy?"

"Okay, I see what you mean." Mark huffed out a short burst
through his nostrils. He finished tying his second shoe. Slowly,
softly, as if calculating, he said, "Sit down, huh?"

He pushed his lips forward, then sat back. "Coach, the thing
is this. If those guys are playing, I'm playing. All there is to it."
He rose without giving the man another glance and started
walking toward the ballfield. "Sit down, my butt."

Stats did not move, letting Mark's choice weigh in. He still
had a great chance, but if he was going to play, he would no
longer be a sure thing. Somehow, though, Stats was not surprised. After all, Mark was a ballplayer. And that's what they
do—play ball.

He watched number nine jog onto the field to join his team.

"Keep him in the lineup, Stats." The coach stood up. "Geez,
I hope he doesn't regret this."

It was a hope Stats shared as well. Even so, he had never
in his life held more admiration for his brother than at that
moment.

Next, he repeated in his mind the last thing Mark had said.
Sit down, my butt.

Stats grinned and stretched his legs out, getting comfortable on the dark green bench. Mark might have meant that as a joke, but as far as Stats was concerned, those were words to live by.

Mark's first home run of the day went to left. His second, though, was an oppo-field beaut, clearing the fence in the right-center gap by five feet. A real power blast. He was having no trouble at the plate that day.

The trouble was in the field.

In the third inning, he charged a red-hot skimmer to his left, which caught the heel of his glove and shot straight up and over his shoulder into center field.

Too hot to handle? Stats thought so. But to be sure, he went to check with Mr. Scorggins, the official scorekeeper, between innings. It was declared an error. With a shaky hand, Stats recorded an E-6 into his book.

Immediately, he checked with the Stat Pack. Since most of the meaningful games were farther west that day, there were no new reports. But for some strange reason, there was a new name.

"What the heck?" Stats shook his eXfyle, then reloaded the page. Same results.

On the top of the list of fielding percentages in the shortstop category, there was another guy with a one thousand mark.

"Who's this Tony Welzer?" asked Stats, echoing his text to the Pack. "Where did he come from?" It had to be some kind of mistake. It would be impossible for another player to gain perfect status.

Soon enough he had his answer. The kid had been in the

second-base category until game time. Having split his defensive duties between short, second, and third, he had only today recorded more innings at shortstop than at any other spot. Thus, he now qualified in Mark's category.

"Oh, great." Should I tell Mark? he wondered. Would he want to know? Or would it cause him to press too hard? He's already made one error.

For the moment, Stats kept the info to himself.

Mr. 2B/3B/SS was one-for-two so far. And based on having a lower number of at bats, the guy, Welzer, could actually pass Mark's average if he got another hit.

When Mark flew out to center his third time up, he fell perilously close to the guy in batting average. With another hit, Tony Welzer could climb to the top of the list of shortstops—in both categories.

A shadow passed over the scorebook. It was Mark's.

"Why're you looking so worried, Freddy? What's going on?"

Stats squinted up at his brother. He could not lie. "Another guy just passed you. At least, he's ahead in fielding and just a few points away in hitting."

"What? You kidding me?" Mark shook his head. "Geez, somebody's having a good day."

That was all talk, and Stats knew it. Mark was doing his utmost to stay loose, treating the news lightly, trying to stay focused.

If only, thought Stats, Mark had just taken Coach Carrigan's advice and had sat this one out. He'd still be perfect in the field.

"Forget about it, Freddy," said Mark. "Seriously. Don't tell me anything else about my situation. I just want to play my game." He strode off.

Welzer's game was moving along faster than Mark's. He was soon two-for-three and had moved in front of Mark in hitting by one point.

It's slipping away, Stats realized. Mark's chance to play at Fenway, to represent America—the spot he owned going into this game—was slowly slipping away.

In Mark's final at bat, he walked. Normally this would not be a bad thing. But today nothing was normal. With the walk, Mark's average froze. That would have been fine if he were still in the lead. But he wasn't. He was still two-for-three on the day and he had needed to gain ground if he were to have even one sliver of a chance.

Then the news got worse. Tony Welzer was now three-for-four, no doubt riding a wave of adrenaline, Stats figured. He sat four points in front of Mark. Four points. That was like a million light-years ahead.

Uncatchable. By anyone.

In the bottom of the seventh, the final inning, Mark stood at shortstop pawing the earth. Could he possibly know what had happened? Had he felt the vibe of sadness that radiated from Stats?

All Mark's team needed were three outs and they would win the game 4–2, but Stats barely felt like watching.

The first batter walked.

"Double play, Mark!" shouted Coach Carrigan from the dugout. "Let's get two right here."

At this point, if not for the scorebook on his lap, Stats would hardly have known he was at a baseball game. But a sad cloud hovering nearby kept reminding him. He was at the worst baseball game he had ever witnessed.

The next guy doubled, but was tagged out by Mark after he got caught in a rundown between second and third.

Though one run came in, the play had emptied the bases and essentially killed whatever rally might have been brewing. One down, two to go.

Nice job, Monty, thought Stats. Way to pitch yourself out of a jam.

When he walked the next batter, Mark started yelling. "Let's bear down, Monty! Get this next guy, right here. Come on now." He shouted across to Jonny Peskovich at second. "Let's turn two, Pesko. Get this game over with."

Monty bore down. And he plunked the next batter in the ribs with a fastball.

Stats didn't even record the play. So Monty falls apart? So Back Bay loses? Something horrible had already happened, and Stats was the only one who knew about it.

He watched with drained emotions as the next hitter bounced a chopper over the mound. Mark had shaded the guy toward the middle, double-play depth, so he was in a good spot, but had to backpedal to reach the high hopper. He grabbed it with his glove hand. At second, Pesko had also broken for the ball, then gave way to Mark and ran behind him.

In a case like this, the pitcher should've covered second, but Monty decided to be a spectator, so no one was there to take Mark's throw. All he could do was race to the bag. It was the only play Mark had, and he got there just before the runner slid in.

Two down. Tying run on third.

So who cares, thought Stats, if we win or not?

His heart hurt as if he were the one who'd lost the all-star spot. Second place. Going nowhere. All because of an error. And there was nothing anyone could do about it.

CHAPTER 35

The following hitter—the Stallions' best—took the next two pitches, both low and away. Walk him, thought Stats. Set up a force at second. It's a one-run game, 4–3. Only the guy on third really means anything. Come on, let's get this over with.

The batter walked. The cleanup hitter did too. Bases loaded. Not exactly textbook baseball, since the winning run was now on second, but still, there was a force play now at every base.

"Let's go, Bums!" shouted Stats, more out of frustration than conviction. "Last batter now. Force at any base. Come on, you guys!"

Into the batter's box walked the catcher, a fire hydrant of a guy with no neck and thick stubby arms. Quick stubby arms. He'd already had two singles in the game, both driven hard through the hole between shortstop and third.

The first pitch sailed high and inside. The guy ducked.

"Throw strikes!" Mark pleaded. "We'll get him out."

The next pitch was inside again. Belt high. The guy turned on it and slapped a hard grounder to the left side. This time Mark had shaded him perfectly, two steps toward third.

He slid across to get in front of the ball. Picture perfect. He brought his hands back against his belt and, with a gentle ease, scooped the ball up.

He sent a nice low underhand flip to Kerwacki, who stood waiting with one foot on third. Jacky Kerwacki, however, possessed a trait that at times presented the guy with a challenge. He had the attention span of a juvenile gnat. The runner from second was nowhere close, but Jacky seemed to be getting anxious. He banged his glove with his bare fist, then lunged out for the ball just as it arrived. The ball bounced off the thumb of his glove before dribbling away behind him.

Mark never broke stride. After the toss, he had planned to leave the field anyway, seeing the third out in front of him. So he continued on and raced past third base, overtaking the ball before it reached the dugout, where he slid to a stop. Cocking his arm, he spun toward home from his knees to gauge the situation. The runner who'd been on third was crossing the plate.

The trailing runner—most likely underestimating Mark's athleticism—had decided to head on home, too, once he spotted the ball bounce past Kerwacki.

About halfway down the line, though, he skidded to a panicky halt, having seen Mark's battlefield pirouette.

For a split second, he and Mark stared eyeball to eyeball, not five feet from each other, until Mark scrambled up and charged right at him. Before the guy could regain his traction, Mark dove, head down, glove out, and slapped the runner on top of his ankle.

The umpire's fist shot up. Three outs.

Stats caught himself hooting and bouncing against the dugout's chain-link fence. The play was that good.

If there was another fifteen-year-old shortstop in the world who could have made that play, Stats would like to see him do it.

After righting himself, Mark flipped the ball toward the mound and came trotting in. It wasn't until that very moment that Stats fully realized what had just happened. The game was not over. It was tied.

By going all out, by almost killing himself to make a nearly impossible play, Mark had done the only thing within his power to keep alive his already-dim hopes of making the nationals. He'd kept the game alive too.

"Who's up?" shouted Mark as he hit the bench, slapping a posse of hands walking past. "Freddy, who made last out?"

Stats did not have to look. "Top of the order's up."

"Okay!" Mark clapped his hands. He showed no acknowledgment of the underlying message in what Stats had just said.

Mark was the number three hitter. He would bat again.

In the top of the eighth, Mark hit his third home run of the afternoon, and it made the other two look average. Dead center on dead red, it flew so high above the scoreboard that even in

Fenway, Stats figured, the ball would have caught a glimmer of light from the fancy John Hancock sign. The Back Bay Bums now led 5–4.

After Mark crossed home, Stats was waiting at the dugout opening.

"You are having a career day," said Stats.

"Hope so," Mark answered, underlining the importance this day might truly have on his future. Too bad the all-star spot was based on batting average and not slugging percentage, because no shortstop had the power numbers Mark had. But when it comes to batting average, a homer is the same as a single.

Stats whipped out his eXfyle and texted away.

A lot had happened since the last time he'd checked in. Welzer had ended the afternoon three-for-four. But he had also made an error.

Hey, thought Stats, nobody's perfect.

Now the bad news. Due to having slightly more chances in the field, Welzer was still in the lead in both categories. In batting, he led by eight-tenths of a point. He led in fielding by four-hundredths of a point.

Sully made the third out for the Back Bay Bums, and they took the field with a one-run lead.

Unless the Stallions could tie this game once again in the bottom of the eighth, Mark was finished. Could Stats even wish for such a thing?

Could Ted Williams drive a ball thirty-seven rows up into the right-field bleachers, 502 feet away?

As the bottom of the inning proceeded, it soon became apparent the Stallions were running on fumes. They had no fight left. The first guy hit a chopper up the middle, which Mark easily handled.

The next guy fouled off three pitches before popping up behind the mound. Mark called everyone off and squeezed it for out number two. Unless there was a miracle—like their number eight hitter clobbering a homer—this game was history. Mark would have no more chances at the plate. He would lose his position on the national team by an eyelash.

Even so, he had played one of his greatest games of all time. Three home runs, two amazing plays in the field, and one bad hop, bad-luck call.

Stats scanned the sky for a hawk. Nothing.

He now became a mere spectator. A "traitor" might be more accurate. His scorebook had fallen to the floor, and he'd secretly begun rooting for the Stallions to score one more measly run.

Tie this game, he kept repeating. Tie this game. Bruce Mombocat, the new Back Bay pitcher, was even wilder than Monty. He misplayed a bunt right back at him, then hurriedly threw it away, letting the batter reach second. Then he walked the guy behind him. Two outs all right, but there were now two runners on base.

No, no, thought Stats. Easy now, Stallions. You just have to tie the game, keep it alive. Please do not win it.

The next guy up swatted a flare line drive just behind third base, lofting perfectly over Jacky's head—a softly served base hit for sure.

Stats shook the fence. Another run! Yes! He then caught himself and froze, trying to keep his excitement secret.

But before the dying quail could fall to the grass, Mark had scrambled to his right, angling deep behind third, and lunged for it, landing with a thump and a roll.

He rose quickly, showing white leather peeking out over the webbing of his glove.

A brilliant, incredible catch. A game-winning, game-ending catch. Three outs. The Bums had won.

And Mark had lost.

It was a long ride home from Stonybrook.

"I did my best, Freddy," said Mark. "Don't take it so hard. Look at me. I'm okay."

"How can you say that?"

"Because I keep telling myself, this ain't nothing compared to what Pops is going through. Or what the Sox are going through. And look at Billee."

"Well, yeah, you're right, but still . . ."

"Hey, dude, I'll play at Fenway someday, promise. You watch. Same way all these other guys get to. I'll work my way up and earn my spot."

"But that's just it. You did. It was a statistical quirk that got the other guy in. He played at second and third over half the time. Those spots are nowhere near as difficult as shortstop. He spent over half the season at two positions where he could knock the ball down with his chest, bobble it, and still throw the runner out at first. It's not fair."

Mark didn't respond. It became clear to Stats that he was done talking about it. In that way, Mark was a lot like Pops. He wanted no sympathy. He wanted to hear no gripes. What's done was done. Time to move on.

Then Stats did something he rarely did. He powered down his eXfyle—his connection to the statistical world. For the first time in a long time, he shut off his phone.

CHAPTER 36

Saturday night, halfway through a game that had already seen two Red Sox errors and two pitchers, the video crew began to set up on the field just in front of Stats and Mark.

"Get ready, Freddy," said a crew member who wore a wide blue tie with big red baseballs all over it. "At the top of the fifth, you're on." He sent Stats a goofy full-tooth grin.

Stats gazed up above the light banks. He knew by now his pursuit of "hawkness" was probably a lost cause—even Billee had more important things to worry about than bringing the "chee" back to the Fen—but he wished that even one small hawk would fly over and land somewhere inside the ballpark.

So far, of course, nothing.

Mark must have read the concern on his face. He shook his brother's shoulder. "Hey, it's okay, Freddy. You're a kid. You don't have to say anything special. All right? You'll be great."

When that "great" moment finally arrived, Stats wondered if the pounding of his heart would be seen through his shirt and shown all over the JumboTron.

"Okay, lights," said the wide-tie guy.

Stats rose.

"In honor of Fenway Park's one-hundred-year anniversary," came the sonorous tones of Carl Beane, the Red Sox public address announcer up in the booth, "tonight's testimonial will be given by the son of one of Boston's greatest longtime public servants, an icon of Yawkey Way, Pops Pagano of Papa Pagano's Red Sox Red Hots, located right outside the ballpark gates. Everyone, please welcome twelve-year-old Alfredo Carl Pagano."

During the polite applause, the production guy handed Stats the on-field microphone.

"Start, start," he said, then quickly looked down at his watch.

Stats saw his face flash onto one of the three huge HD video screens serving the ballpark. He bent his head and turned toward home plate to keep from being distracted.

"Hello, my friends of Red Sox Nation," he managed to say. A hush fell over the crowd. Stats could hear people shushing each other, pointing to a video board. The production guy was winding his hand, urging him to move it along.

"Like he said, my name is Alfredo, but most people call me Stats because I love the statistics of baseball and I like to keep score." He held his scorebook in front of his face. "This is my scorebook. I bring one to every game I go to."

For reasons he could not comprehend, he heard a smattering of applause, which then grew so loud he had to stop.

It made him grin. "Thank you. I didn't know what to say tonight, but Pops—my dad—always told us to follow our dreams. So if I could, I'd like to tell you one of mine."

Of course, he didn't have to wait for anyone's approval, but he paused a moment anyway.

"When my grandfather came here from Italy in the 1930s, he wanted to be of service to his new country. He tried to join the army, but he had a bad heart, which kinda runs in our family. So he bought a hot dog cart instead and rolled it around the town and especially to Red Sox games outside Fenway Park. To him it was the most American thing he could do."

Stats paused again, noticing he had begun to lose his train of thought. He felt the pounding of his heart in his ears.

"Um, our family has held season tickets for over seventy years—seventy-two to be exact, counting this one. Sorry, I'm always exact. Anyhow, we've seen all the ups and downs. Like my brother once told me, when other people gave up, we still showed up. And during those days when the bandwagon filled up, we were always happy just to bring the food."

It had by now become obvious that this testimony was going on far longer than thirty seconds. Already the producer had circled his finger to signal "Wrap it up," which had only distracted Stats. When he started again, the guy made a sharp chopping motion with the side of his hand against his palm. Stats looked away.

"Me and my brother, Mark, sit in the same seats my grandparents sat in. The same seats my mother and father used to sit in. When my mom died, my father stayed outside mostly. I think it's because he couldn't bear to come down and sit here without her. This baseball park has sort of turned into a sacred place to our family. I think a lot of people feel that way."

Finally the guy with the baseball tie drew his fingertips in a cutting motion across his throat.

"Uh, Freddy," the man said, approaching quickly and reaching for the mic. "Thank you, thank you. That was great."

Mark stood up and put his arm across the guy's chest, cutting him off. "Hey, let him say what he's gonna say. This is baseball. There's no clock."

The man started to protest. "But he's—"

"Hey," said Mark. "He's speaking for us now. Stand back. Relax."

Stats heard that very sentiment echoed by several other fans nearby.

The man backed off.

Stats regained a measure of calm. "So anyway, here's my dream. When we walk through the halls of Fenway Park with all the memories of all the guys who played here, I dream that we remember each of them and we honor them and we honor the guys who are on the team right now, because someday they will be memories, too. And we come and watch them do their best. And we watch what we say." He paused, realizing that thought applied to him right now.

Turning to face the people behind him, he said, "I dream that each time we walk through these gates, our hearts will be happy. Whether we're coming in or going out, it doesn't matter. Because this is our family. If we don't pull for each other, who will? And even though my mom is gone, and my pop owes a ton of money for all the bills, and even though I have a bad heart like my grandfather and have to go to the hospital sometimes, I can come here and feel happy. Because . . ."

He paused to make sure the words fit the picture in his mind.

"Because this park is the heart of Red Sox Nation. It has the kind of heart I always wanted, one that's forty thousand people strong, who love their team, even though some days it sure doesn't seem like it, but you do. You do. And in my dream you show it. Because in my dream, when I pass through these gates, this balky heart I was born with turns perfect. Sometimes it lasts for a few innings, sometimes it lasts all week. But when I hear my friends in the stands yell and boo at my friends on the field, it breaks my heart. And I don't like it."

At this moment, Stats realized the fielders had stopped warming up, had ceased any movement at all. Every one of them stood facing him.

"So I hope someday it'll be like in my dream in here, and my heart could stay like it is when I come to Fenway forever. Thank you. Sorry I took so long. Um, play ball."

It was as if the sea tide of normal sounds had pulled back and receded deeper than anyone had ever witnessed, leaving a strange void, which then gave way to the roaring tsunami of sound that followed.

The crowd clapped, whistled, cheered, and stomped. Though to be honest, Stats barely heard any of it. Why had he gone on so long? Boy, they must be glad that's over with. He should've just stopped when the guy asked him to.

The first sign Stats saw of any impact his speech might have had on the Fenway faithful was the lack of signs. By the start of the inning, gone were THE BREEZE BLOWS IT AGAIN, WANTED: SOMEONE WHO CAN PLAY THIS GAME, and the one Stats particularly disliked depicting a Red Sox cap sitting atop a tombstone that had the letters R.I.S.P. on it.

And though that sign would've proven useful later on in the seventh when the Breeze popped up with two outs, leaving two Runners In Scoring Position stranded on second and third, it never appeared.

Some hecklers still heckled, but not as much, and their catcalls were often followed by shouts of encouragement from others. Yankees fans, well known to be boisterous and bellicose, kept their comments geared toward congratulating their guys on a play well executed. The most amazing thing, however, was when Announcer Bouncer used his megaphone voice to calmly and loudly announce, "Red Sox, we love you. That's from the kid's heart, and we're all *The Kid* tonight."

The whistles and cheers that followed came through this time, loud and clear.

"Freddy," said Mark in his softest brotherly tone, "you knocked it out of the park."

CHAPTER 37

Alfredo Carl "Stats" Pagano had not planned on being famous. If he had, he would have worn better clothes. But that night, before the game was even over, dozens of fans had approached him and asked, rather politely, he noticed, if they might take a picture of him. And then they would ask for one *with* him.

Soon, Mark was directing traffic in and out of their small section of seats. That lasted well after the bottom of the ninth, when Dusty Doretta hit a sharp liner to second for the final out, with the tying run on third.

Before Stats left the ballpark, Bull Brickner approached him with another request.

"Hey, Statsmo. Lookit, some guys in the press box are wantin' you to come up and take a few questions. Whaddya think?"

He thought it would be scary, but fun. He went.

The first few questions were easy. What school do you go to? What grade? Do you play baseball? How many games do you go to a year? Who's your favorite player?

"My favorite player is Billee Orbitt, but I like them all. This is my favorite team so far."

"Even though the Spacebird just got sent down?"

"That doesn't matter. He'll be back."

"What do you like about him?"

Stats decided to give that one a little more thought. He dug for an answer he deemed worthy of the subject involved.

"Billee gives hope to a lot of us who are only just sort of normal and also sort of weird." When they all laughed, he added, "I mean weird in a good way."

"For example . . ."

"Well, for example, he doesn't watch TV, and neither do I, except for Sox games. He plays baseball, which I don't, but we are both huge baseball fans. He likes the history, and I like the numbers." Stats searched around the top of his head for better examples. "Oh, and we both wish we could ride in a spaceship."

When that brought head nods, he added, "Also, we both believe in the power of harmony. I like to see it between people, and he likes to see it between everything on the earth. He calls it balance. I call it setting things right so everyone gets treated equal. But it seems like those ideas make us different from most people."

"How so? How do you think most people see it?"

That was a good question. It made him pretend to be a normal kid for once and try to see things from that point of view.

"I don't think they mean to hurt anybody, exactly, but most people see being out of balance in the equality department as okay. Especially if things are going their way. And if they get the chance, they would rather tilt things their own way than to give everyone else the same chance."

The reporter chuckled a bit, looking around at his colleagues. "You don't see that as being a natural survival instinct?"

"I don't see that as being fair."

From the other side of the room a woman asked, "You mentioned your family has had some difficulties. Medical and financial. How extensive, or how deep, is your family debt? Do you know?"

Stats did not feel that question was appropriate. Their family's business was private. He certainly was not going to mention that Papa Pagano's was up for sale. But he hated to disappoint, especially when it came to numbers. He remembered when Billee was asked the same kind of question, regarding his rookie-year salary, and Stats used that exact answer as his own.

"Let's just say it's somewhere in the low six figures. Next, please."

"Okay, folks," Mr. Lucchesi interjected, looking a bit uneasy. "Last question." He pointed to a woman who raised her notebook. "Heidi."

"Alfredo, what advice would you give the Red Sox right now based on your own personal experience?"

It was only then that he happened to catch a quick glimpse of his brother, Mark, standing in the very back of the room. Grinning.

"Well, first I'd say nobody's perfect." After that brought a laugh, he added, "Then I'd say if you want to climb as high as you can, don't look down. You've already been there. Look up."

CHAPTER 38

The *Boston Globe* is the most widely read newspaper in New England. The Sunday sports pages, online and in print, are read by hundreds of thousands of people all over the world. On that Sunday morning, Stats Pagano's picture was on the front page of the sports section, next to an article all about him and his message from the night before. In a rectangular box under the article was his little speech, word for word.

Upon reading the first paragraph or two, he thought he sounded so dumb, he could not even finish it. His thoughts seemed so random and disconnected. Pops told him his talk was brilliant, but that was Pops, who promptly went out and bought twenty copies, wiping out the supplies at the corner Dunkin' Donuts and the sidewalk machine in front of the Sam Alone's Bar down the block.

That morning, Pops posted the *Globe*'s picture of Stats on a small makeshift easel at the hot dog stand. It seemed to make a difference in the pregame moods of the patrons who shuffled up and ordered what Stats figured could be a record number of hot dogs for one day. And though his heart panged for a visit from Billee, for just a small reminder of the good ol' days, he couldn't wait to total the numbers for Pops.

The night before, the Sox had lost a close one. Sure, they showed a lot of spark, but to hear the customers stepping up to the counter, you might think the Sox had just made the play-offs.

"Hitting's coming around. That's one good thing."

"Pitching will, too, once they realize they don't have to throw a shutout to win."

They were intelligent comments by genuine fans. They could just as easily have made snide remarks, pooh-poohing the team, but for some reason they had chosen not to.

"I was there last night," a number of people told Stats. They all congratulated him on a fine job. He could hardly look up with all the attention beaming down on him.

Some customers showed off the signs they'd brought that day.

THE BANDWAGON STARTS HERE
ANOTHER GREAT DAY AT THE FEN
WE'LL BE HERE AT THE END!

Stats thanked them all, but he was so nervous about being in the spotlight all morning, he mislabeled several orders, using the wrong wrappers, and filled other orders twice. No one seemed to mind.

The real test of this change in attitude would come, he knew, during the game. This was, after all, the Yankees series. Four games. And the Sox had just lost the first two and were riding a *six-game* losing streak. They were bound to win some soon, sure. The percentages alone told him that. But these next two seemed urgent.

Just before game time, as Mark rushed around to help clean up, Stats walked out into the street. He looked up. Please, he prayed, just one hawk. Just one wing flap. Just a little "chee."

Sadly, there was nothing.

Coming back around the front of the stand, he did notice one interesting development. The tip jar was stuffed.

Now, that happened every once in a while. If the Sox won a big game and shot into first place late in the season, the next day the overall good mood was often reflected in bigger tips. But the Sox were eleven games out of first place at the moment.

"How do you figure that?" Mark asked, eyeing the take.

"I don't. You know me. I only deal with things that make sense."

"I'll tell you why," said Pops. "Mark, you're using better manners up front. You both hustle. You're on top of things. People appreciate that. Like they say, you're gonna catch more flies with honey than vinegar, eh?"

"Yeah, I guess," said Mark. "But I catch more flies with my glove."

He deserved the whack on the hat that Pops gave him for that one. But Pops had also given Stats an idea.

Before he left the stand, Stats shook open two plastic zip bags. He then placed two Chili Billees into each bag.

"Pops, I'm starving!"

He resealed the bags and put one in each of the front pockets of his hoodie.

The seesaw game that followed caused Stats more worry than a blowout would have. Each team had held the lead twice, but the Sox went into the ninth trailing the Yanks by one, 8–7.

The fans never gave up. As the Sox came in to hit, the rally caps came out. Everyone turned their hats inside out, and those without hats put food boxes on their heads. Some did both. They clapped and stomped for each pitch.

With two outs in the bottom of the ninth and runners on first and second, the Breeze walked up with a perfect chance to redeem himself after last night's pop-up. And as if the crowd had willed it, he belted a shot into the right-field gap. It immediately reminded Stats of a classic David Ortiz walk-off bomb he'd seen on so many highlight DVDs.

When the Yankees' center fielder jumped high above the fence top to pull it back in, however, the cheering roar turned into the loudest groan Stats could ever recall.

The perfect Hollywood storybook ending had eluded the Fenway fans, and for a moment they all stood in shock. The Breeze reeled around second, then slowed up after seeing the umpire's fist.

It seemed every eye in the park was on Rico Ruíz.

And the crowd roared again.

The ovation lasted over a minute. These were the fans Stats knew so well. No, their team had not won, and, yes, they had dropped a heartbreaker to the dreaded Pinstripes, but these baseball lovers had witnessed a game. They had seen a go-for-broke never-give-up spirit in the hometown nine and they liked it.

When Stats turned around and looked at the full-house crowd, not yet heading for the gates, one small red and blue sign caught his eye.

LOOK UP

Before leaving the park late that afternoon, Stats took a detour to the outside stairway leading to the upper deck. Yes, he thought, that's exactly what I'm going to do. On the street-side landing, about ten feet below the roof, he stopped and faced away from the park.

He was not looking for anything. He was getting into position. He felt the wind on his back.

"Mama, they're going to operate. I guess you know that." He let his eyes roam the sky. "Okay, just this. Am I going to die?"

He waited. He imagined what it would be like to be shed of this awkward, poorly functioning shell he lived within. He imagined what it would be like to walk around with a battery-operated heart.

Neither option scared him.

Staying just as he was seemed worst of all.

"Mama? Will you be there?" He felt a warmth rise inside of him.

"Okay, good. Now, Mama, tell me when and where."

He heard no voices. That's not the way she did it. Instead an impulse came to him, clear as the Boston sky.

"Straight up, straight back," he felt. "Two on the east side of the press box roof, two on the west."

"I hope this works." He removed a plastic bag from his left pocket. Looking up, he flipped two Chili Billees onto the east-side roof.

He stepped to the west side and did the same. Afterward, a puff of wind cooled his face, lifting the brim of his cap. And that was all.

CHAPTER 39

At 11:30 that Sunday night, Mark's phone rang. Of all the times to forget to shut it down. Who was calling so late?

Mark squinted at the display. "Who's Dewey Larson?"

Stats sat up. "Oh, that's for me. Sorry."

Mark tossed him the phone. Stats opened it. "Hey."

"Hey, your phone goes straight to voice mail."

"Yeah, I know. What's up?"

"Where you been?"

"Asleep. It's the middle of the night. Why?"

"No, I mean—never mind. West Coast just reported in—twenty-four hours late. I think they held off until they could double-check their numbers for the whole season."

"So? That doesn't change anything. Everyone knows who the leader is."

"Oh, and so, you what—just unweb yourself from your cyberspiders? Nice guy."

"Look, I'm hanging up now. I don't want to talk about this."

"Fine, but one question. Did you even see the L.A. results?"

"L.A.? That didn't even matter. That guy was way behind. Welzer won."

"Says you. Welzer was three-for-four. L.A. went five-for-five. He passed up Welzer."

"As if it matters. Look, I'm sleeping. Talk to you later." Stats shut down the phone.

"What'd he want?" asked Mark.

"I don't know. He's one of these guys who only sleeps three hours a night, so he's only half there, reality-wise. Sorry."

"S'okay." Mark rolled over.

Stats walked to his laptop. He was awake and curious enough about L.A. to at least check it out. He was happy, too, that it seemed a pure shortstop had won the spot.

In batting average, Welzer edged out Mark by one point. That was not news. He also barely lost to L.A. by one. But there it was on the ballfield graphic. Mark still led in fielding percentage.

How is that possible? How did Mark pass Welzer in fielding? They both had one error, and Welzer had more total chances, so the error hurt him the least. It didn't make sense.

Then, as if he were smacked by a bat, Stats understood. After studying the numbers, he realized why the shortstop category had changed completely. It all came down to what Mark had done at the very end of the game. Five put-outs and one assist, accounting for all six outs in the seventh and the eighth innings—the two meaningless innings that Stats never bothered

209

to record in his book. Though he now realized Mr. Scorggins had recorded them all—and reported them.

Due to those six extra chances, Mark's final fielding percentage had been nudged up ever so slightly from .995 to .996. Welzer now sat five one-hundredths of a point behind Mark. And since neither player led in both categories, the YMBL went to its tiebreaker—slugging percentage. In that category, Mark creamed the poor guy.

Stats switched to the YMBL all-star position graphic. On the green and brown animated sketch of Fenway Park, all of the top YMBL national players were listed in blinking bright blue letters, according to their positions.

At shortstop, the name read "Mark Pagano, Boston."

Stats woke early the next morning and jumped right out of bed. He fired up his eXfyle on the dining room table and set about designing the perfect way to let Mark, who was still sawing logs, learn the good—no, the amazing—news by fashioning a baseball card of Mark wearing a custom-designed YMBL All-Star baseball cap.

After making a few final adjustments, including Photoshopping a big wad of chaw into Mark's left cheek, he uploaded the image. Then he designed the text.

MARKO "Sit Down My Butt" PAGANO
BATS: R(eal good) THROWS: R(eal hard)
POSITION: Shortstop-aroony
HOME FIELD: Fenway Park

Stats sent the baseball card to the printer back in the bedroom. He arrived in time to hear Mark complaining.

"What are you doing now?" He snugged the pillow around his ears. "That printer is so loud. Need to get a new one."

It was not loud for long. Zip-zip. A quick image on photo paper, then a reinsert for back-to-back printing of Mark's up-to-the-instant stats, a quick trim job, and presto!

Mark stared at the finished card. After Stats proved once and for all that, as goofy as it looked, the card was no gag, Mark just sat and gawked at it.

He would be playing shortstop in a real game in the magical confines of Fenway Park.

CHAPTER **40**

On Monday at Papa Pagano's, Pops had another son to gloat about. Though he didn't particularly like the way Stats had rendered Mark on the baseball card—that is, the cheek full of chewing tobacco—he nevertheless easeled it, front and center, next to the *Globe*'s article on Stats.

The crowd was just as enthusiastic today as it had been on Sunday. Why? Two breaking news items had caught the attention of Red Sox Nation.

First off, it seemed that Cedro Marichal had left Sunday's game only in part because of his performance. The other reason was due to a hyperextended knee, which caused him to change his landing mechanics so much, his control went haywire. Fifteen-day disabled list for Cedro.

That left a huge hole in the Red Sox pitching rotation. Enter—or, rather, re-enter—Billee. In what might prove to be the world's quickest rehab assignment ever, Billee was recalled from Pawtucket.

At first Stats couldn't understand, since technically, once demoted to triple-A, a player had to stay at least ten days before he could be recalled. But Billee had never officially reported to Pawtucket. Since he was not due until Monday, and it was only a one-hour drive away, Billee's locker had not even been emptied.

Two news items? No, actually three. Billee's last start, he would be first to admit—and *did*, actually, in the morning paper—had amounted to nothing more than a "long workout," lasting only about twenty minutes. Thus, he was in all actuality the most rested Red Sox starter on the roster. Therefore, on Monday night, for the fourth and final game of the Yankees series, Billee Orbitt would take the mound.

Would this alone explain the enthusiasm on display along Yawkey Way that morning? Not likely, thought Stats. Sure, an upcoming Billee Orbitt game had always lifted spirits, but he had not been his old self in so long, it could not be the reason for the upbeat mood.

Before Stats and Mark rushed off to catch the start of the game, Pops said, "This may be it, boys."

"May be what?" Stats had already lifted the escape hatch and was ready to leave.

"While you're inside, I'll be meeting with a broker representing a prospective buyer for the business. He says he has a top-notch offer for me."

"What's top-notch?" Stats wondered.

"Well, we're asking a hundred and eighty-five thousand dollars. Top-notch, to me, says he's got a hundred and eighty-five large in his pocket. But we'll see." Then Pops waved at the air in front of him. "Hey, hey. It has to be done, and the sooner the better."

"Are we really going to reopen the store?" asked Stats.

"As I say, we'll see. I don't know anything yet. I just need to get out from under all this."

"Whoa," said Mark. He had not been paying attention. He had the tip jar contents spread out on the back counter. "This is our biggest haul yet." He looked up. "People are putting twenties in there."

That caught Stats's interest. "How much does it come to?"

"This is unbelievable. Pops, there's over five hundred dollars in here."

Stats hustled over to look. "Hey, we could pay off the whole debt with just another"—he paused to calculate—"uh, two hundred and sixty-three days like today." His smile dimmed when he realized just how long it would take to reach that many days in home baseball games—over three full years.

Mark scooped up the paper money. "Pops, you take all these. We'll take our twenty-five in change. At least it'll do some good."

Pops took the money with a crooked frown. "Uh, look, leave the change. You boys go enjoy yourselves." He handed each of his sons two twenty-dollar bills. "We'll talk about this later."

CHAPTER 41

Billee started off strong Monday night. The game was being broadcast nationally, and the crowd knew it. They were with him during warm-ups, and they exploded in cheers when he struck out the leadoff man.

Then came the fireworks. The next batter went golfing after a forkball and sent a screamer down the third-base line that never rose above four feet high. This wasn't just a frozen rope. It was frozen smoke.

And even Stats, as close as he was to the ball, could not quite believe Wadell Fens, the third baseman, snagged the liner as it zoomed past.

That was the second out, and the play garnered a standing ovation.

Then the number three hitter drove the third pitch he saw so high and deep into center field, Stats immediately saw 1–0 flash into his mind.

The skyball flew toward the center-field "nook" four hundred and twenty feet away, the deepest part of the park. Luckily, the center fielder, Teddy Lynn, raced to the warning track and hauled it in only inches shy of the fence.

"Just a long out!" cried Mr. McCord. Others agreed as the enthusiastic crowd offered its second standing O of the night. But those in the know knew. Since the Yankees were timing Billee's pitches this well, this early in the game, in order for the Red Sox to have any chance at all tonight, they would have to do it with their bats.

"Better put some runs up, boys!" yelled Announcer Bouncer. "We're gonna need 'em."

Stats penciled in the F-8 and drew a double line indicating the inning's end. Three up, three down for Billee in the first, but it was not pretty.

"Sox better have their hittin' shoes on," said Mark as the Yankees took the field. "Billee's getting hammered."

The hammering went both ways in the early going. But by the end of two, only the Red Sox had crossed the plate, and they'd done it twice.

As Billee took the mound at the top of the third, with a 2–0 lead, Stats noticed something in the sky above the right-field seats.

Three hawks circled in the late twilight.

Look up, Billee, *look up*, he thought.

Billee, though, was deep into his pre-inning ritual, smoothing out the mound, walking around it to pick up the rosin bag and bounce it off the wrist of his pitching hand four times.

Two things now kept the Boston fans in a roaring mood, fully supporting their starter. He had fanned the last batter in the second, and due to a diving grab and a kneeling whip-throw by Rico Ruíz from out in, basically, shallow center, the Yankees had yet to reach base.

Before Billee's first pitch, a distant cry echoed through the ballyard.

"Chee! Chee!"

Billee paused a moment. Had he heard it? He sent a sideways glance toward Stats and slowly stepped back off the pitching rubber, setting the ball into the palm of his glove. Then he looked up.

It was the very moment one of the hawks that had circled the field touched down on the press box roof. It was entirely possible, Stats thought, that he and Billee were the only two people in the park to notice.

In his scorebook, on this batter's third-inning line, he wrote an H. When the hitter grounded out to second base, Stats circled it.

From that moment on, Billee Orbitt seemed to possess a rhythm, a tempo, a balance that Stats had not remembered seeing since his rookie year.

"It's going to be a good game," he told Mark.

"Hope so."

"Know so."

Mark looked over at him, let his eyes linger with eyebrows up, huffed, then turned back to the game.

Stats would not again mention the status of tonight's contest nor his personal view of Billee's performance for the rest of the evening. He couldn't. No one who knew anything about baseball could speak of it. For Billee went into the ninth pitching a no-hitter.

Actually, it was more than that.

Billee Orbitt was pitching a perfect game.

CHAPTER 42

No one on the bench had spoken a word to Billee since the fourth. Stats could see from where he sat that Billee did not go down the tunnel between innings, as he sometimes would. For eight straight innings, he went to his usual spot at the end of the bench, watched the game with his glove still on, parked upon his knee, and no one came close.

A no-hitter is a fragile being, Stats knew as well as anyone. It is borne of purely spiritual parts. In fact, not a bit of it even exists until it is delivered, fully formed, at the end of the game.

A perfect game is an even higher, lighter being. Some say it is almost pure light. That's how Stats saw it. Its effects will linger long after the typical no-hitter has lost its glow. The perfect game is baseball's rapture, a radiance that travels through all time wrapped around a no-hitter. Its creator is never forgotten. In 132 years of Major League Baseball, only 20 perfect games have ever been recorded.

Billee was on the cusp of immortality. Three outs to go.

At this point, advantage Yanks, even though they were losing. The pressure was not on them to break the game open. It was on the pitcher to keep its perfection preserved.

The leadoff batter stood in and took the first pitch, low and away. He then took the next pitch, which kissed the dirt. The third pitch sailed high, and the crowd rustled with the nervous shuffle of a single mind in distress. Three balls, no strikes. Would the first runner reach base on a walk?

The batter stood patient. Billee breathed deep.

Strike one. Strike two.

Then and only then did the hitter look as if he had come to the plate to hit. He stepped out, took a sign from his coach, and dropped the bat head to the dirt between his feet. He then proceeded to eye Billee while rubbing the handle of the bat between his hands like a fire starter. Ready now, he stepped back into the box.

Billee talked to the ball—that is, as most fans now knew, to himself through the ball. He set it softly into the palm of his bullskin glove. The lefty began his reeling rotation. His right leg swung round, pointing to the center fielder, then his whole body unwound, falling forward, his shoulders momentarily squaring with the first baseman as his left hand lifted out of the glove, his whole left arm a bullwhip cocking, then cracking, over the shoulder, bringing the ball, snapping it as his right foot touched the earth and his left leg came down to stomp it.

Low, at the knees. The batter swung, driving a sharp two-hopper to short, and the Breeze had all the time in the world to step up, grab it, pound his leather palm once, crow-skip, and fire a strike to first.

One out.

Then the crowd, in its perfect wisdom, shouted "Ruu-eeze," loud and long, as if that one play and that one player were the only things on the collective mind of this collective baseball fan who was perched on the edge of history.

The next batter, a pinch hitter, tried to bunt his way on, fouling it off, and the wrath of Ted Williams fell down on him.

"Bush! Bush!" The angry cries went up, and ridicule tinged every word after that.

"Gutless jerk!"

"Stinking coward!"

Undeterred, the batter showed bunt again, but pulled back in time to hear the umpire call the butterfly pitch a strike.

By then the hook had been set. That is, the hitter set up. After seeing the floating leaflutz, he was now no match for Billee's ninety-five-mile-an-hour heat. He flailed at it anyway, beginning his swing at almost the same time the fastball smacked into Burly's mitt. Strike three.

Around the horn the white ball flew, with no player daring to look another in the eye. After that, to a man, they merely hung their torsos, spit on the red clay, and pounded their gloves with a common fury.

Then, twisting, they let "bull horn" fists tell the story. Each infielder held a pinky and a pointing finger high, purely for show, signaling to the outfielders what they had already known forever.

"Two outs!"

Stats could not imagine what Billee must be thinking in the midst of this miracle-making moment. Nor could he have dreamed what the next hitter was thinking when he jumped on the very first pitch.

A slow untamed, unassuming chopper full of topspin bucked and bounded down the first-base line.

First baseman Sandiego Gunsalvo charged in to field the ball as Billee dashed over to cover the bag.

Stats knew. Mark knew. Anyone with any baseball knowledge at all felt an instinctive flash of fear, knowing what a topspinning bounder could do upon hitting earth or leather. Watching Gunsalvo bend and glove it cleanly, they now worried that a left-handed pitcher was running toward first base while facing home plate with his glove hand trailing behind.

The throw would be lefty to lefty, heightening the drama still, for the ball would come almost from the mound.

Gunsalvo's flip was quick and good. The race was close. Billee's foot found the base with an intentional, but stuttering, double-stomp just as the ball snapped his glove, just as the runner crossed the bag.

Even with the angle Stats enjoyed from across the diamond, he could not be certain.

Had the ball arrived in time? Whose foot landed first? Three huge JumboTron boards showed the replay a dozen times or more. And they always ended the same way. Out, out, out at first. It was a perfect game.

CHAPTER 43

The crowd, as they say, went wild. The team did, too. They would not let Billee retreat to the dugout, but descended upon him as a massive hugging mob that wobbled amoeba-like from the pitcher's mound to home plate with grown men jumping upon one another as if they'd just won the lottery and the World Series combined.

Eventually Billee did squirm free, but only enough to shoulder-bang his way past third base and stumble toward the front-row seats in section 71.

It had been 108 years since any pitcher had thrown a perfect game for the Red Sox, that feat being performed by none other than the old-timer, one Mr. Cy Young, in 1904. And he, of course, had not done it at Fenway, which had yet to be built. Since then, the ball club had survived decade upon decade of slightly more "imperfection" than anyone would have liked, but the drought was now over.

That curse, broken.

Lunging toward Stats, Billee picked him up out of the stands, hoisting him onto his shoulders, as Stats clasped his ankles and rode upon his friend through the ruckus clinging like a rodeo rider for dear life. Once again, he sat directly over Billee on a magical night at Fenway. They headed back toward home plate, toward the park's power point. Billee must have had something in mind.

"What an awesome game!" yelled Stats, and he would have said more, but what was the use? The clamor and roar swallowed all voices—or, rather, rolled them into one. For tonight, all were united, in heart and joy.

Arriving at home plate, Stats used his elevated status to survey the ballpark. Once again he enjoyed being so far above it all, having always been so much "below it all." As if by a secret prompt, the rest of the Red Sox players began to back away, forming a small circular moat of respect and admiration around the pitcher and his young friend.

Billee doffed his cap and began a small, slow turn to the crowded house. Facing the scoreboard, Stats finally saw himself on the video display.

Embarrassed, he leaned down. "What should I do, Billee?"

"Just tip your cap, Stat Man. And smile."

Stats checked his head, but touched only hair.

"I lost my hat," he reported.

"Then wave!"

He waved with all his might. As Billee continued his slow spin, Stats saw another video board. And he soon saw what had become of his hat. Mark had it—or he did for a moment. Mr.

McCord seemed to take it from him and, as the nearby cameras recorded the scene, he slipped a few dollars into the up-turned cap.

Then he passed it along. The video view zoomed in to show only the hat and a stream of hands as it was passed along from fan to fan. And filled.

Another display showed another section of Fenway and another group of fans starting their own passing hat, priming it with a few dollars and sending it along. And another. And pop-corn bags. And beer cups. And Cracker Jack boxes. Row after row. Section by section, fans added donations to whatever vehicle passed their way and passed it on.

To be honest, it took Stats a minute or so to surmise the intent of the money-givers. The Jimmy Fund, perhaps, or some other worthy cause? Stats wondered if word had leaked out about his operation tomorrow.

Either motive would have made sense. But he soon realized neither one was the case. As the newspapers would tell it in their morning editions, the Pagano family had given much to Boston baseball over the years, and most recently, Stats had given his heartfelt inspiration to them—one that seemed to have helped beyond measure. And now that the Paganos needed a bit of help from their neighbors—this family of fans—they were only too happy to pitch in. And, of course, that fit. Boston town is a baseball town, and baseball is a team sport. So naturally, when someone on the team needs help, you help your team.

Billee finally placed Stats back on terra firma.

"Let's go inside," the lefty said, giving one last wave as they stood at the edge of the dugout. "I'm starved."

He dangled an arm, pulling Stats against his leg, and they descended the dugout steps. Funny thing was, Stats still felt as if he were floating in the sky, high above Fenway, swirling with the stars and moon.

CHAPTER 44

As Billee once said, there is so much we don't know and there's so much we can never know.

For example, no one could have known Billee's perfect effort would begin a twelve-game winning streak. Or that the Sox would go on to regain first place by the end of August.

No one could have known the forty thousand "hat-passers" would chip in enough to stuff a duffel bag with an amount that surpassed any earthly demand the Pagano family currently held. The average contribution came to about five dollars and, as Mark often said to Stats, "You do the math."

Pops did, and Papa Pagano's was no longer for sale.

But perhaps the most difficult thing for anyone to have known was that when Stats reported for his pre-operation prep at six A.M. on Tuesday morning, there would be complications.

"Do you see that, nurse?"

"I do, but I'm not sure it's accurate. The chart says he's bradyarrhythmic. But with a pulse like that?"

Doc Roberts studied the digital monitor a moment longer. "We'll need to get his father in here."

Neither Stats nor Pops could have known the heart monitors that day at Children's Hospital would record a strong, even pulse, showing full oxygenation into his entire cardiovascular system, and a complete lack of symptoms suggesting any heart defect or damage at all.

No one present wanted to use the word *miracle*. No one had to. Ask the Fenway faithful, ask the Red Sox, ask the town of Boston or the hawks above. And they would all tell you. Of course there's nothing wrong with this kid's heart.

Haven't you been paying attention?

Stats was dressed and out the door well before noon. He was at the game that night and at each one for the remainder of the home stand, including the Orioles game on Saturday in which Billee was again scheduled to pitch. But before that game came another.

The American YMBL all-star squad had a date with destiny in a championship game versus their counterparts from Japan, and Stats, as usual, had a front-row seat.

And an extra ticket.

Luckily, he had a taker. Early that afternoon Pops Pagano made his way down the ancient aisle, step by step, stopping along the way—not only to take in the ballfield and the young players hustling through their infield-outfield drills, but to take and shake the hands of so many old friends who had missed the man with the hot dog grin and the twinkling eyes for these past four years.

"Welcome back, Pops."

"Great to see you, Angelo!"

"Hey, there he is! About time, Pops."

But it took Mr. McCord to put a fine point on the occasion as he rose and shook Pops's hand. "Well, now, Mr. Pagano. Welcome home."

That day both home teams came away victorious. That night two old friends met way out in the bull pen to sit under the moon and stars and ponder the fates.

The hawks were back. Video evidence soon filled the blogs, as did the story of balance Billee told about the mission he and Stats undertook to rescue the ancient ballfield from further decline.

Fenway Park became the only baseball venue in America to add a line about hawks to their cautionary warning on the flip side of each ticket.

"Part of the game," explained Billee. "People have to understand. Just like home runs and foul balls."

"So, are we going to win the World Series?" asked Stats. "Every year from now on?"

"I don't know about that," said Billee, rising from his chair and heading for the gate. "But I think we should be okay until around 2090."

"Why 2090?" Stats joined Billee in a slow amble across the outfield grass toward the Red Sox dugout.

"Well, because we're due for about eighty-six years of good luck, wouldn't you say?"

"Starting back in 2004?"

"Yep."

"To balance things out?"

"You got it." He ruffled Stats's cap. "Come on, I better get you home."

"Yeah, okay." A moment later, he asked, "Do you think the chili dogs really did it? Do you think they actually brought the hawks back?"

"I'd put 'em at the top of my list."

"Oh." Stats could not hide his disappointment.

"What's wrong, Stat Man?"

"Well, just to be safe, don't you think you should fly me around Fenway Park a few more times?"

"Oh, I do. You bet. I was just thinking that myself."

And they walked on, upon a lush and magical green carpet ready to transport them anywhere.

DISCUSSION QUESTIONS

1. Consider the concept of balance. What meanings could balance have in baseball? In life? Who in the novel has it?

2. Consider the notion of "inter-connectivity." What does balance have to do with connectedness for a ball club? For an individual? For a family?

3. To Stats, walking across the infield at Fenway Park was a sacred act, and he had the sense that he was on holy ground when he did so. Why? What is holy ground for you?

4. Stats considered Billee to be a genius because of the way he makes connections between many things. What other person that the world calls a genius made connections? What connections were they, and how did they benefit the world?

5. Billee makes a joke saying their problems are caused by a "hawk's nest monster." First, is it true? Second, what does this description also sound like?

6. Billee comes close to defining friendship when Stats is tethered to the balloons and asks Billee why he chose to be Stats' friend. What did Billee want out of the friendship? Did he get it or would there always be some sort of imbalance between him and Stats?

7. To be assured of his ranking, why didn't Mark make the safer choice and sit out the game? Did he do the right thing? What quality did that decision show in him? Do you know of anyone in history who took a similar risk?

8. Why is Mark's story as a ballplayer interwoven into the greater story of Fenway Park? What does it add? What does it demonstrate about the sport?

9. Why was Stats' speech so moving to the fans? What did they appreciate in it? How did they respond?

10. Why is Pops so beloved by his sons? Think of several reasons. Why is he beloved by the Red Sox Nation?

11. How do you account for Stats' healing? Is it a miracle or is it a natural outcome of his thinking? In the story, what elements may have contributed to it?

FOR MORE QUESTIONS, PLEASE VISIT THE AUTHOR'S WEB SITE AT WWW.JOHNHRITTER.COM.

Turn the page for a sample of
John H. Ritter's
first exciting baseball book!

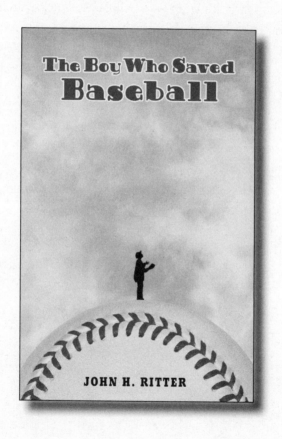

1

Tom Gallagher sensed the ghostly calm even before he opened his eyes. In a hill town known for its harsh and wild winds, the morning broke without even the whisper of a breeze.

Tom had hoped today would be as ordinary as possible. He'd woken early, dressed, and finished off a plate of his mother's *chorizo con huevos,* as he usually did on a Sunday morning. Then he'd walked outdoors to pay his friendly old neighbor, Doc Altenheimer, a friendly old visit, as he usually did on Sundays. He'd stopped to pick up the paper at the foot of Doc's long driveway, as usual. But today, Tom was planning to do something *un*usual.

"Hey, Doc!" he called as he hustled toward the huge white house. "Padres are in third!"

"Well, what do you know," Doc called back. "There's hope yet, isn't there?"

The eighty-seven-year-old apple rancher sat at a yellow kitchen table set smack in the middle of his long front porch. He leaned out and slid a chair over the wooden deck boards.

"Come have a seat, Tom." Doc talked like he moved, slow and easy. "Good to see a friendly face. My gosh, with that Town Hall meeting coming up tonight, everybody and their brother's been by here lately, trying to sell me on one fool plan or another."

Doc's words hit Tom two ways. First, he felt instantly guilty, since he was here to do the very same thing. Tom wanted to make sure, once and for all, that Doc understood this whole land-development scheme some people were pushing for was a bad idea.

Then he felt double nervous. Tom had spent all week working on a little speech. Never in his twelve and a half years had he done anything like that before—to write out a speech ahead of time in order to remember what to say when the time comes.

Should be easy, right? All he had to do was to step up and deliver his pitch, just the way he'd practiced it. Well, not so easy for Tom Gallagher. Even though his father was a teacher—who spoke to crowds—and his mom was the school librarian—who read to crowds—Tom was far more comfortable keeping his thoughts to himself, even with his friends.

"Yesterday," said Doc, "the mayor stopped by for about the hundredth time. Him and that new banker fellow from Texas who's been buying up all the land." Doc opened up the sports pages with soft, tremoring hands. He spread out the baseball section so Tom could read him the scores.

"Funny, ain't it, son? Now that it's all come down to me, it looks like I took over being the most popular and the least popular man in town at the same time."

Tom puffed out a small laugh. He'd heard that phrase lots of times in these hills, but never in regards to Doc. There was a shadowy former pro baseball player named Dante Del Gato, a one-time hometown hero, who officially wore that title. Nowadays, the man was practically a hermit, living on top of Rattlesnake Ridge.

"After the mayor left," Doc continued, "the Historical Society came calling. Daisy Ramirez and that bunch of busybodies. Tried to tell me that this old, broken-down baseball field was a *historical monument*. Oughta be preserved. Well, I told 'em, it's history, all right. Soon as I sell the land, it'll be history." Doc laughed. "They didn't appreciate that."

Sell the land? *Wait a minute!* Just yesterday Tom had reassured the other ballplayers, saying, "Trust me on this. Doc won't sell. He's a baseball man. And he loves these hills. He used to walk up his ridge, spot the perfect big-leaf maple tree, trim off a branch, and make his own bat from it. He's on our side."

Now Tom wondered how he could've been so wrong. "You mean, you might—you might actually—"

"I'm leaning that way, son," said Doc. "Trouble is, I've gone round and round on this deal so many times, I feel like a windmill in a windstorm. But tonight's the big night, isn't it? Got to let everyone know tonight." He took out a handkerchief, held it against his mouth, and coughed.

Now, Tom told himself. Tell him now! Don't wait another second.

Tom scooted his chair closer. He gripped the seat bottom. Then he scooted back. He closed one eye and tried to focus on his mission. Then he closed the other. He saw the words, but he could not make himself speak.

"I ain't a fool, Tom. Sure, it means more traffic and noise

and bulldozers kicking up dust all year long. But all in all, I think it'll be good for us. This place is dying, son. And as far as I can see, there's only one way to pump life and spirit back into Dillontown. Open up the highway, build new roads and new homes, and bring in more jobs. Those builders did nice enough work down the hill. I expect they'll do the same up here." He tucked away his handkerchief. "Wouldn't be selling 'em my land if I didn't. Jumpin' jackrabbits, what do I need with six million dollars, man my age?"

That nearly knocked Tom off his chair backwards. *Six million dollars?* That much? Well, Doc, he thought, you could give it to me. But Tom had never considered the idea that a man might reach a point in life when even a million dollars was not important.

And Tom had seen the new ballpark down in Lake View Mesa, the shiny chain-link fences and store-bought grass, all neat and trim. He'd seen the new baseball camp whose summer team began an annual challenge game against the Dillontown camp three years ago. Some challenge. Each year, they'd beaten Tom and the Dillontown Wildcats by at least ten runs.

Maybe brand-new and improved *was* better.

For the next half hour, Tom pored over the sports pages for Doc, their usual ritual. He'd call out each game result and the box score highlights, and each time, Doc had something wise and thoughtful to contribute.

"Don't count them Pirates out of it just yet. Those young players've got more heart and hunger than all them overpaid millionaires combined!"

Tom nodded, but in his brain all he could do was yell at himself. *Why didn't I talk to him sooner?* Why'd I keep putting it off? And why can't I tell him now that I think we're losing the greatest ballpark in the world, with a hundred years of baseball swirling its walls and a right-hand batter's box that holds the very same dirt that Dante Del Gato once dug into and spat into on his way into the world-record books?

Slowly, Tom found the next score, the Yankees game, and was about to read it out when Doc spoke up again.

"You know, I've been here all my life. My wife and son, God hold them close, lived and died right here. Even in hard times, this town's been good to me." He set his elbows on the table and laced his fingers together. "And I just hope to return the favor. That's all."

Tom sat back and stared off into the distance. From Doc's front porch, he could see the spires and crosses of several churches rising above the scattered rooftops of the town below. He could see the shops on Maine and Mercado, the little adobe post office and Town Hall, and La Plaza de Oro, where a cluster of old ladies in white scarves stood feeding the birds before making their way to Mass.

Closer, near the apple groves and farmlands, he could see the ancient baseball field—Lucky Strike Park—built on a dry lake bed a hundred years ago by Doc's father and a gang of crusty gold miners, including Mr. "Long John" Dillon himself, the founder of the town.

Doc still owned Lucky Strike Park, but more importantly, he owned a total of 320 acres of prime real estate, which was key to the whole deal. Doc's land was where the golf course would go, where the best homes would be built, and where the new lake had been planned—a lake that would drown the town's baseball field under fifteen feet of water.

Doc coughed again, wiped his mouth, while his eyes seemed fixed on empty air about halfway to the orange trees on the edge of his front lawn.

"For fifty-five years, I delivered just about every baby born in this town, Tom, including you. So I figure I can deliver the town this one last gift. A new park and a chance for a new life."

Tom's stomach wrenched tighter. He lowered his head. No sense now saying anything. Doc had made his decision and he'd made his peace with it.

Ever since the early 1900s, the Altenheimer family had leased Lucky Strike Park to the townspeople for a dollar a year. This summer, the 100-year lease was up. And over that 100 years, Dillontown had shrunk from 5,000 people down to 559, give or take. Meanwhile, to the west, an ocean of red-tiled rooftops—houses and malls—had crept along the land, coming closer and closer, like a pool of blood oozing up out of the earth itself.

"Once those builders put in a spanking-new field, Tom, it'll be a whole lot better for your team, don't you think? Better facilities. Better equipment. My gosh! Look what it did for those boys down the hill."

For some reason, hearing that fired up a spark in Tom. At the same moment, a breeze began to stir. "Those guys aren't so great," he said. "Just because they got a fancy park with batting cages and everything doesn't make them such great ballplayers. Our field's just as good. And we like it!"

The east wind gusted up and rustled the paper on the table. Tom slammed his arm down to catch it. Then he said something that surprised him as much as it seemed to startle Doc. "Shoot, we could stomp those guys like a bush on fire any day of the week."

Doc pulled back and smiled. "Well, you haven't done it yet."

Tom folded his arms. "Still, we could beat 'em. If we really wanted to. Like the Pittsburgh Pirates, like you said, we got heart. We do. And hunger. Those other games just never meant anything, that's all."

Doc sat a moment longer. "I like your spirit, Thomas. Your age, I was the same way." He took a black pen from his pocket. On the sports page margin, he began to write. Doc often left Tom with a few words to ponder, "words of encouragement," he called them. This time he wrote, *Even in the dead of night, the sun is always shining.*

He replaced the pen. "Nice to hear you speak up, though. But the plain fact is, times've changed. I'm sorry, Tom. It's just too late."

Read on for additional scenes from *Fenway Fever*! These excerpts provide a peek inside John H. Ritter's writing process and show the directions he considered as part of the story's journey to the final result.

EARLY MORNING JUNE 20–21
BEFORE STATS GETS OUT OF BILLEE'S CAR

"Stat Man, I'm going to tell you something that may sound strange."

Stats nodded, resisting the obvious comment. "Sure."

"In one sense, having your mother die at an early age is a lucky break."

Surprisingly—at least to himself—Stats could not offer a solid retort. Billee would never say something cruel or heartless, so he considered the concept. Stats had, in fact, always felt as if having an invisible mother nearby, watching over him, was a great benefit. It was one of the few things he shared with Mark, who was as much a friend and guardian as a brother, and he knew of no one else who enjoyed that magical paradigm which he, by now, took for granted.

Was that what Billee meant?

"Lucky, how?" asked Stats.

"For example, no kid with ordinary parents could possibly understand or take to heart the things I tell you. But a boy who believes in magic can see a bigger picture."

"Magic?"

"Believing in the unseen, the unknown, where not everything has to be proven to you. I lost my dad when I was fourteen. But I know he's always there."

"What people tend to forget is that an ending is also a beginning. With the game's last out, you begin thinking about tomorrow. After the last game of the season, you begin a countdown to spring. That with death comes a rebirth into a new world we don't know much about."

"That's why I don't believe anyone really dies," said Billee. "We just turn the corner and start our next journey."

"We round the bases," said Stats. "And head for home."

Billee turned his head toward Stats. With a calm smile, he nodded. "That's right. And if we don't touch 'em all this time, there's always next time."

"There's always next time, even if we do," said Stats.

Billee let his gaze fall. "You can bat around forever, can't you?"

"Theoretically. Yeah, you can."

AT END

"Billee, I got a great name for the curse we're fighting. It's about the red-tailed hawks, right?"

"Yep."

"Okay. Then we'll call it the 'Curse of the Red Hox.' Stats smiled broadly. "No pun intended."

"None taken."

"But do you like it?"

"Kid, I'm out of ideas. It'll have to do."

⚾ ⚾ ⚾

"Now I got one for you," said Billee. "What kind of nefarious creature would climb up and steal a hawk's nest with eggs in it?"

"I don't know. What?"

"A hawk's nest monster."

"That's bad. That's not even funny."

They laughed and laughed.

⚾ ⚾ ⚾

IN HOSPITAL, AFTER DREAM TALK WITH BILLEE

"How do you guys know all this stuff about me?"

"We are from a parallel world."

"I knew it! I *knew* there really was such a thing."

"Your scientists have theorized the concept for several years now."

"I know. Michio Kaku and all those guys. I love to read all about that stuff."

"Yes, you do. That is why we felt we could approach you with our request."

"Wow, that's amazing. But can I ask you one question first?"

"Yes, you may."

"Will the Sox win the 2012 World Series?"

"At present, the possibility/probability vortex in the Earth plane suggests that the Boston Red Sox will enter the play-offs and be victorious at every level."

"Wow! Even though it looks sort of iffy right now?"

"This is true. However, nothing is certain. You must remember, the Boston Red Sox have won every World Series every year since 1903."

Oh, great. These ET guys don't know diddly-squat. "No, I'm sorry, they haven't. It's actually just been only a handful of times."

"Again, this is true. In your current timeline, they have won seven such events. But you must understand, there exist an infinite number of parallel timelines, dimensions, if you will; and in a vast number of these, the Red Sox win the World Series every year."

"Wow."

"In fact, in a majority of universes, Babe Ruth plays his entire career with the Red Sox."

"Oh. Whoa. That's a lot to think about." He paused. "What about a guy like Johnny Damon? Is he still playing for the Sox?"

"Perhaps in a few planes. But most Red Sox teams did not sign him but rather signed a player known to you as Matt Damon, who was far more loyal. And he had a better arm."

"Get outta here!"

"We are gone."

And they were.

JUNE 25
AFTER-GAME CELEBRATION

He did not need the Jumbotron to see one hat being passed. All he needed was to see one player, Dirk Scooter, the Yankee's shortstop, emerge from the visitors' dugout, hat in hand.

A hat filled with cash.

He passed it to the usher, then disappeared back down the tunnel. Yes, even the Yankees had joined the cause.

IN HOSPITAL, READING IN BED

"Hey, Mark."

"Yeah."

"What does 'ample bosom' mean?"

"What kind of book are you reading?"

Stats showed him the cover. "A lady from the hospital gave it to me. By an English guy. Dickens."

"And he has those words in there?"

Stats nodded.

"Well, it means. . . ." He stopped and looked around the room. He leaned forward. "Means . . . a fairly, you know, big chest on a woman."

"Boobs?"

"Yeah."

Stats lowered his eyes and nodded again, saying nothing.

"Do you like the book?" asked Mark.

"Now I do."

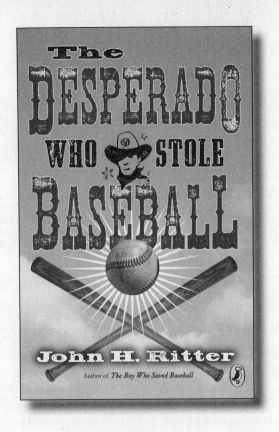

The fate of a Wild West gold-mining town rests in the hands of two individuals. One is a twelve-year-old boy with a love and instinct for baseball unmatched by any grown-up. The other is the country's most infamous outlaw, on the run and looking for peace of mind. Together, they pair up to prove that heroes can emerge from anywhere. John H. Ritter brings the Old West to life in this prequel to his breakout success, *The Boy Who Saved Baseball*.